I0651726

Wynter Frore Knight

Our Vicar

A novel

Wynter Frore Knight

Our Vicar
A novel

ISBN/EAN: 9783337052416

Printed in Europe, USA, Canada, Australia, Japan

Cover: Foto ©Andreas Hilbeck / pixelio.de

More available books at **www.hansebooks.com**

A Novel.

BY

WYNTER FRORE KNIGHT, B.C.L.

IN THREE VOLUMES.
VOL. I.

London:

SAMUEL TINSLEY & CO.,
10, SOUTHAMPTON STREET, STRAND.
1879.

[*All Rights Reserved.*]

PREFACE.

THE characters attempted to be portrayed in this story are, with a qualification, imaginary. There is a slight substratum of fact in some of the incidents, and the author trusts that if any of the actors in the original scenes should recognise it, they will kindly pardon the colouring and manipulation to which it has been subjected to serve the purposes of a novel.

One main object of the book is to show the dangers and difficulties which may surround a man of keen sensibility and honourable feeling when brought into subordinate and close relations with one of the opposite character. If in so doing the author has created in the Vicar of Pollington a being which has no real existence, he is content if it be conceded that such a one may yet be possible.

CONTENTS OF VOL. I.

Contents.

OUR VICAR.

CHAPTER I.

THE VICAR AND HIS FAMILY.

'I THINK Plainton will do if we can secure him, my dear,' said the Vicar to his wife.

'I have done all I can to draw him. I pointed out in my note that the bishop spoke highly of him, that the neighbourhood was attractive, and the people pleasant. I hope it will fetch him. It ought.'

'Well, I hope so. But he has a sister living with him, I think you said? I wonder what she is like?'

'Ah! there's the danger. Curates' women-folk do all the mischief in a parish. We must get them to luncheon, and then we shall see.'

The Vicar of Pollington was a remarkable man in his way. He was the son of a literary man, and the grandson of another. The great-grandfather, like many more distinguished men whose lives are recorded in history, had come up to London with half-a-crown in his pocket. What he did with the half-crown is not known, but it is known that the owner obtained employment in the office of a weekly newspaper, and by diligence and ability at last attained to the editorship of the publication whose interest he had so long served. His name was Enoch Hatter. His son was named after him, and so was his son's son. His great-grandson, the subject of this faithful history, continued the family name. He was sent to Cambridge on leaving school, and after a somewhat distinguished career, entered Holy Orders. Having served three or four curacies in the country, he took duty in the West End of London. Here he met with the family of the Pipps. The Pipps were well connected, and very proud of their lineage, having very little else to boast of. They supported the Conservative interest. Young Hatter reflected, that as he was without powerful relations, an alliance with the Pipps might be useful, especially as there was a good deal of Church patronage in the gift of some remote connections of the family. But Hatter was by conviction a Liberal. He determined, however, to sacrifice his political principles to the good of the Church, and to support the Conservative side, should he be successful in obtaining the favour of one of the three daughters of old Mr. Pipps.

The Misses Pipps were not handsome. The eldest was tall and slim, with rather hard features. The second was short and stout, with a good-natured, vulgar face. The youngest was somewhat like the eldest, but less hard-favoured. They were not distinguished for amiability, whatever else might be their graces and attractions ; and their intimate friends, in playful allusion to their eccentricities of character, nicknamed them, Envy, Hatred, and Malice—Hatred being the appellation of the eldest. The brother of their Vicar was said to be the first to give them these ornamental titles, and on being severly remonstrated with by his sister-in-law, replied, in a shocked tone :

'Well, Mary, I wonder how you can condemn anything that is in the Prayer-book ; for that is where I found the names, I did not invent them. I shall tell Tom that you are taking up with the Evangelicals, and beginning to speak evil of our incomparable Liturgy.'

For some inscrutable reason, unknown to the historian, Enoch Hatter made love to gaunt Hatred. He went about his work in a way peculiar to himself—slowly, subtly, surely. At first there was great opposition amongst her friends, but as Hatred would have her own way, they at last gave in. Soon after his preferment to a small living,

they married. The fruit of this union was
two children—a boy named after his father,
and a girl, Hester. About a year after the
birth of the latter, Hatter received, through
his wife's connections, the living of Pollington, a pleasant, river - side village in
Surrey.

At the time when this story begins, their
eldest child, Enoch, was about eight years
old, whilst Hetty was two years younger.
Hetty had very early begun to assert the privi-
leges of her sex by persecuting her brother,
notwithstanding the difference of their ages.
Young Enoch was a meek and quiet boy, and
quite unequal to the task of contending with
his passionate sister, who was always backed
up by her foolish parents.

The boy was not sorry, therefore, when
it was determined to send him to school at
his uncle's, who owned and conducted an
'establishment for young gentlemen,' in the
suburbs of the metropolis.

Hetty, who could bear no rival near her
throne, thus reigned supreme all the year

until the holidays came round, when she re-
newed her battles with her brother.

She looked a some that delicate child, and was
very like her father in features and character.
Unfortunately, she had an extremely fractious
temper, and as both parents were doatingly
fond of her, she was humoured and spoiled in
every way. Her eccentricities of temper
soon became known in the village, and were
commented on with the eloquence charac-
teristic of village gossips. The boys of the
parish called her Kicksy, because they mostly
saw her in the act of stamping or kicking.
Whilst the more relentless of the Vicar's
critics affirmed that the child simply in-
herited the chief characteristics of both
parents, and was consequently without the
trace of a single good quality. This was
hard upon the poor child, who, however, was
happily unconscious of their uncharitable
remarks.

The conversation with which this chapter
opens, took place immediately after the Vicar
had written to the Rev. Pawley Plainton to

offer him the curacy of Pollington, about to become vacant through the resignation of the present curate on the occasion of his marriage.

After one or two letters had passed, Mr. Plainton and his sister Margaret came to luncheon. When they arrived at the Vicarage punctually at the appointed hour, they found that the Vicar and his wife were both out. Plainton thought it a little odd, but supposed that some important parish business had probably detained them. In half-an-hour's time they came in.

'Eh—eh—how do you do, Mr. Plainton ? Eh—glad to see you. It is rather a wet day. Eh—eh—hope you won't take cold.'

These observations were uttered in a hesitating, gasping tone, whilst he hurriedly shook hands with his guests. Plainton thought at first that he liked his face. He had a shapely head. The forehead was high and intellectual, and the features looked like those of a student. But Plainton did not quite like his manner. It was too tentative and hesitating. The lower part of the face, too, was uncomely. The mouth was coarse and sensual; the lips did not meet well. But the oddest peculiarity of all was the shifting action of the eye, and the strange, changing glitter as it moved. Hatter did not look frankly at his visitors, but gave them short, quick glances, occasionally dropping his eyelids so as to scan them unobserved. What Plainton most disliked was, that he received his sister in a cold, constrained manner; addressed no observations to her; but frequently looked at her furtively and obliquely with that strange, uncanny glitter, which caught the curate's attention as soon as Hatter entered the room.

The walk from the railway had been a wet one. Margaret's jacket was glistening with the rain-drops, and her thin boots were wet through. But neither the Vicar nor his amiable consort took the slightest heed. Whilst the Vicar in his hesitating way was descanting on the beauties and advantages of the neighbourhood, a loud squall was heard from the adjoining room. Mrs. Hatter disappeared for a few moments, the squall subsided, and the gruff voice of the Vicar's wife was heard instead speaking in a subdued but authoritative tone.

'Now, Hetty, be good at once, and come and speak to the gentleman and lady.'

'I shan't!'

'Sh! sh! come at once.'

'I'll kick them.'

The door opened, and Hetty appeared led firmly by the hand by her mother. The child stood and scanned the visitors with a defiant and inquisitive gaze, and having satisfied herself that they were nobodies, shook her shoulders in an unmistakable manner.

Mrs. Hatter, in a persuasive tone:

'Shake hands with Mr. Plainton, Hetty.'

'I shan't.'

Mrs. Hatter, authoritatively:

'Go at once, and shake hands, and say "How do you do?"'

Hetty gave two steps forwards, and then, with great dexterity for so young a practitioner, expectorated with considerable force in the direction of the visitors. Probably fearing reprisals, she immediately followed up her attack by a protective and prolonged squall, and was forthwith hurried off from the scene of her exploit.

Plainton and his sister were greatly embarrassed, and, in order to pass the incident over without commenting on it, the former observed in an unconcerned manner :

'It's a fine day—I mean, except for the rain.'

'Eh—eh—yes,' gasped the Vicar. 'Perhaps Miss Plainton will not mind being left alone a few moments while I speak to you in my study.'

Plainton rose and followed the Vicar, who led the way to a small room at the back of the house. The atmosphere of this retreat was laden with the stale perfume of very strong cavendish tobacco. On the mantelpiece were two or three dirty pipes ; whilst on the table lay a new book just out from the press, and beside it some proof sheets of the

Vicar's great work, upon which he had spent sixteen years of his life, and which was shortly to appear. It was . called 'The Extinct Dialects of the Zulus.'

We shall not trouble our readers with all the details of this interview. Mr. Hatter began by eulogizing Plainton's past work and expressing his decided opinion that the curate was eminently qualified to fulfil the duties offered to him at Pollington.

' The neighbourhood is delightful—you can have any amount of boating on the river— the people will receive you with open arms ; and if you should desire to marry, there are more than fifty heiresses living in the place, each with not less than seven hundred pounds a year. They are all most eager to be married.'

' I should not come here with the intention or desire of marrying,' remarked Plainton coldly, for he was getting to dislike more and more the worldly tone . Mr. Hatter was adopting.

He had heard as yet nothing about evange-

lising the poor, nothing of mission work, nor of
the parish machinery and organisation. Mr.
Hatter had dealt almost exclusively on the
worldly advantages the new curate would be
likely to reap from accepting the proffered
curacy.

'Eh—eh—certainly not,' ejaculated the
Vicar in reply to Plainton's remark. 'But—
eh—you will of course desire to teach them
better things; to be, in fact, an apostle
amongst them.'

There was just the faintest flavour of a
sneer as he uttered these words, but the
curate could not tell if it were intentional or
accidental.   Then, suddenly changing his
tone, and giving one of those quick, oblique
glances Plainton had noticed at first, he
observed :

'Eh—eh.   There is your sister, you know.
She is not a—eh—girl, you know; and—eh
—eh—you might like—eh—you ought, of
course, to consider her. If you contemplated
getting her married, ample opportunities—eh
—would be offered here.   We—eh—ought

not to overlook the requirements of those—
eh—who are dear to us.'

Plainton was silent through sheer vexation.
Could this be the eminent writer of whom
he had heard so much ? Was this the philo-
sophic teacher of the age, whose contributions
to the weekly *Scrutator* were so much admired ?

' No, it cannot be,' thought Plainton ; ' he
has mistaken me, and perhaps, by a pardonable
concession to my supposed weaknesses, is
mentioning first the things that would be
likely to interest me.'

The curate then inquired particularly into
the spiritual condition of the people, the
attendance at church, the work in the schools,
and the charitable institutions of the parish.
Here the conversation assumed a more satis-
factory tone, and Plainton received in a few
minutes a clear and encouraging statement
on all these points, though, as it afterwards
turned out, a far from accurate one.

They then went in to luncheon. It did not
last long, for there was very little conversa-

tion. Hatter and his wife ate with extreme voracity, and appeared to have little time or inclination for anything else while the food was before them.

'This is often the way,' said Plainton afterwards to Margaret, 'with great thinkers. Their minds are so concentrated on their literary efforts, that even while they eat they are planning new theories and preparing for new discoveries.'

'Of a medical character, I should think,' rejoined Margaret. 'For I do not wonder at the increase of diseases of the dyspeptic and biliary type, when I think of the disgusting way in which Hatter and his wife swallow their food.'

'You are rather severe, Maggy,' observed her brother deprecatingly.

'And so ought Hatter's indigestion to be,' she replied.

One little incident, however, broke the monotonous clatter of the knives and forks at the luncheon. Mrs. Hatter had given a piece of cheese to Hetty's dog; but as it was larger than the portion assigned to that young lady, she resented the apparent preference, first, by throwing her spoon at the unfortunate cur, and then her plate at her mother. She was immediately, as if by invisible hands —the maid had come unperceived behind Plainton's chair—removed from the room.

'Eh—eh,' gasped the Vicar—'little Hetty is a lively child, and rather given to pleasantries—eh—to amuse the dog.'

As soon as his visitors had left, Hatter observed to his wife :

'Plainton will do very well when we have sat upon a few of his Quixotic notions about the poor ; but his sister looks a Tartar.'

'Well, I don't know. She has rather an incisive way of speaking of things ; but I should think she is quite manageable.'

'She looks consumptive, that's one comfort,' said the far-seeing Vicar ; 'and I should think would most likely go to a better place before the year is out. Did you notice her cough?—dry, hacking, and consumptive, most certainly.'

'I am not sure about that. Her cough was probably owing to her wet feet. She is certainly delicate; but I doubt if she is likely to go just yet.'

'Ah! that is the worst of those thin, little women. They never go when they are expected to do so.'

On their return home, Plainton and his sister discussed the interview. Margaret's remarks were brief and to the point.

'I don't like one of the lot. Hatter is a shifty, and I should say an unscrupulous man. His wife is rude, gaunt, and ugly.' The child is comical enough in her way, but is irretrievably spoiled.'

'Oh! Margaret, how uncharitable it is of you to talk in this way! Remember the name he bears, and all that he has written. His pamphlet on the difficult question of " Poor Relief" is unsurpassed.'

'I do not care for what a man says. I go by his acts, his looks, his manners. Words are *but* words.'

'I am not satisfied myself. There are one

or two things, I think, extremely unsatisfactory, which I must have explained before I decide one way or the other. I will write at once.'

'Well, you will, of course, do what you think is right. But I am quite sure that if you go, you will repent of it.'

'Did you get any conversation with Mrs. Hatter while I was in the study?'

'Oh! yes. She is much more communicative and frank than her husband. She did not speak very highly of the parish, and seemed to think that the people, both rich and poor, are difficult to manage. The former, according to her account, are comfortable, indolent, and half-educated; while the latter are a drunken set, and never go to church.'

'Dear me! I received quite a different account from her husband. How odd!'

'Well, you must add both together, and divide by two. But Mrs. Hatter certainly looks anxious and worried, and may never have taken to the place. I don't know.'

CHAPTER II.

THE NEW CURATE.

PLAINTON wrote to the Vicar of Pollington on the matters which seemed unsatisfactory. Amongst other subjects, he inquired as to the length of the curate's annual holiday, upon which nothing had hitherto been said.

He received what appeared to be, on the whole, full and careful replies, except on the last-named subject. On that the Vicar wrote a long note, stating how very necessary a rest was to every one; that he trusted Mr. Plainton's work in so beautiful a climate as that of Pollington would in itself be a rest; and with regard to any change of air and scene Mr. Plainton might require, if there were any difficulty about it, he would himself 'share the difficulty equally' with his curate. The salary was to be £130 per annum, guaranteed by the Vicar, of which amount £30 was supposed to be raised by means of an annual sermon preached in the church on behalf of the Curates' Fund.

Plainton at first refused, but at length, after further correspondence, accepted the curacy.

In the week after Easter, he and his sister took up their abode at Pollington, in a cottage facing the village-green, of which Mrs. Evans was the landlady. The three rooms they rented were small and ill-furnished; no others were to be had, except at a rent quite beyond their means. When the curate had unpacked his books and arranged them as well as he could in the confined space allotted to him, he found himself enclosed in very scant quarters. To get into bed without pulling down his books on his head required long practice and considerable dexterity. When once in, he was unable to move again,

even to turn round, for fear he should send
his arm through the window, or shake down
his over-loaded shelves.

When Plainton and Margaret came down
to breakfast the morning after their arrival,
they found a fine, salted tongue on the table,
and what looked like a bottle of medicine.
Beside it they discovered a kind, but somewhat ill-written note, stating that the tongue
and chest-embrocation were sent with Mrs.
Chine's compliments and best wishes. The
wrapper of the bottle was inscribed in the
same hand, to the 'Rev. Pawley Plainton,
M.A. : to be well rubbed in before going to
sleep.'

'I hope,' said Margaret, 'that the tongue
is not an emblem of the lady's chief cha-
racteristic.'

'Now, do not let us begin our happy so-
journ in Pollington by being censorious. I
rather look upon it,' said he laughingly, with
a preliminary flourish of his knife, 'as a type
of the work I am to do here, stirring up the
people to great things by my unadorned elo-

quence, and bestowing it impartially upon rich' (here he placed a substantial slice on Margaret's plate) 'and poor' (placing an equally ample portion on his own).

'I prophecy that Mrs. Chine will soon give us the benefit of hers,' said Margaret. 'But perhaps Mrs. Evans can tell us who she is.'

Mrs. Evans was interrogated, and said :

'Oh! you'll soon know Mrs. Chine, miss; for she's about the parish all day, and talks with everybody.'

'Ah! I see,' thought Plainton; 'one of the right sort—energetic, unselfish, and of a true missionary spirit.'

'Is she a married lady ?' asked Margaret.

'She's a widow, miss.'

'Oh! I suppose she is one of the district visitors ?'

'Yes, miss; leastways, as far as the poor'll have her. But many of 'em shuts their door agin her, as they say she's a mischief-making old cat. But then they knows no better, miss.'

'Ah! that will do, Mrs. Evans, for the present.'

And the landlady retired.

The first few weeks were occupied in receiving and returning calls, in getting acquainted with the inns and outs of the parish, and in arranging work. The population was large and very varied, ranging from a 'cabinet minister to an agricultural labourer,' to use the Vicar's expression. The middle-class predominated, consisting of city merchants, stockbrokers, chiefs of government offices, retired army and navy officers, and a sprinkling of professional men.

No doubt the attractions of the river, which was very pretty about here, would account in a great measure for the number of wealthy people who had taken up their residence in Pollington and its neighbourhood.

The cabinet minister mentioned above was Mr. Secretary Davenport, who had married Lady Carmine, a wealthy widow and a leader of fashion. Mr. Davenport came regularly to church; but Lady Carmine, as the Vicar assured Plainton, could not get dressed by eleven o'clock in the morning, and consequently was compelled to stay away. She had, however, proposed, that Mr. Hatter should make the morning service one hour later, when she thought she could manage to come sometimes.

Plainton had many interviews with the Vicar in the little study already described, to receive instructions in parish matters. He almost always came away with a heavy heart. He was more and more dissatisfied with Hatter's way of looking at men and things. His plans were subtle, and his observations acute; but he,ever seemed to be trying to get the better of his parishioners in some worldly matter. And then he spoke of them in such a cold, calculating way, as if they were so many puppets, to be used only for his own pleasure or profit. Plainton also wondered, again and again, at his strange manner with himself. The Vicar did not look at him while speaking, if he could avoid it ; but very frequently the curate discovered him taking searching and furtive glances, as if he would read to the very bottom of his soul.

A few weeks after Plainton had settled down, Mr. Hatter supplied him with a list of the principal parishioners, against a large proportion of whose names he observed a black cross, and asked what it meant.

' Eh—eh—they are persons who are dis-affected towards me, and who—eh—will require careful and skilful manipulation on your part. If they speak against me, as they will, you will know what to do. Eh— eh—I quite rely on your judgment and—eh —good sense.'

Plainton was sorry to find that the black list contained the names of those with whom he had become most friendly.

' By-the-bye,' continued Hatter, ' I observe that at the Relief Committee you ask questions which are sometimes a little awkward. Eh —eh—it is right to tell you that the Relief Committee is only a blind. I take good care

the members shall have no power. Mrs.
Hatter and myself are the real Relief Committee, but it is just as well to have a dummy
committee to bear the obloquy of anything
we do which is not popular, and it also lets
the churchwardens imagine they have a great
deal to do in the disposal of the offertories
for the poor; but we determine beforehand,
at the Vicarage, what we mean to do, and
then we make the Relief Committee sanc-
tion it; so it is best for you not to ask
questions. Mrs. Hatter will tell you all
that is necessary.'

There was much more work to be done
than the new curate had anticipated. Mrs.
Hatter's estimate, so far as the poorer portion
of the population was concerned, was not far
wrong. There was a great deal of drunkenness, and consequently a proportionate amount
of pauperism and immorality.

The Vicar's health, it appeared, was very
indifferent. In the winter and spring he was
obliged to go abroad for six months, and he
usually spent a month or six weeks in Scot-

land in the summer and autumn. But these
facts Plainton did not learn until after he
had come to live in the place. Hatter had
assured him that the work was to be equally
divided between them. As a matter-of-fact,
he found that the Vicar could seldom preach,
owing to his weak chest, and could never
visit (so he said) for the same reason.
Consequently the sermon every Wednesday
evening fell to the curate's lot, as well as,
occasionally, both sermons and the children's
service on Sunday.

There was a lay missionary at work under
the direction of Mr. Hatter, whose stipend
was paid by the congregation. His name
was Elijah Humm. The Vicar spoke of
him in the highest terms. Plainton did not
take to him. He was a hard-featured, vulgar-
looking man, badly educated, and dirty and
greasy in appearance. Plainton strove hard
to overcome his repugnance to the man;
'for,' as he said to Margaret, 'some of the
Apostles were unlearned men, and taken
from a low station in life.'

'Yes,' she replied, 'but I can hardly imagine that they smelt so strongly of rancid oil as Humm does.'

The curate worked on month after month with vigour and earnestness. He held cottage lectures for the poor, and instruction classes for the Sunday-school teachers. In the special church seasons, such as Advent and Lent, he held devotional meetings in the school, in addition to extra services in the church. In all this labour he was ably seconded by the Langleys, who had worked most assiduously in the parish for years, receiving nought but discouragement and obstruction from their eccentric Vicar.

It may be convenient here to give a brief account of Mrs. Langley. She was the widow of the first Vicar of Pollington, after its separation as a new parish from the old town. She had led a blameless and saintly life, never spoke ill of any one, and what is more, never seemed to think that people could do wrong except by some mistake. When she spoke to Plainton of a man and

woman who were living together in her
district without having first sought the
blessing of the Church, she said, in her slow
and stately manner :

'You see, Mr. Plainton, they are very
poor and ignorant, and I doubt if they knew
any better at the time. It was quite a
mistake, I feel sure ; and I think, after a little
talking to, I shall be able to get them to see
their error.'

Besides Mrs. Langley and her daughters,
the curate received substantial help from
Fred Monmouth, a middle-aged Oxford man,
who held a night-school at his own house in
the winter months, was Secretary of the
Provident Society, and Treasurer of the
Working Men's Club. Wherever anything
good was going on, Fred Monmouth was
sure to be found. Yet he worked in so quiet
and unobtrusive a way, that few people,
except those immediately concerned, knew
of his benevolence and self-denial. Plainton
found his calm, unimpassioned judgment
invaluable ; especially as he himself, being

of a sensitive and somewhat enthusiastic disposition, was not always able to see things, which moved his feelings very strongly, in their true proportions.

CHAPTER III.

THE VICAR'S GARDEN-PARTIES.

It was the Vicar's custom to give three garden-parties during the summer months. It enabled him, he told Plainton, to speak to all the most influential people in the parish in a single afternoon, and both saved him the labour of calling on them, and the expense of having them to dinner. He always made a point of Plainton being present to help him to entertain his visitors. They were not very brilliant gatherings. People came mostly because they were expected to do so, and were afraid of Hatter's spitefulness if they did not; but there was very little social intercourse amongst the guests. The Botts could not think of mixing with the Chubbs, and the Snobbies were far beyond either. They managed to tell themselves off into cliques, and pass away the time in gossip until they could with decency withdraw. There was but one subject upon which all the various groups were agreed, and that was intense dislike of their hospitable Vicar.

The first time Plainton appeared at these strange gatherings, he walked about surveying the scene with mingled wonder and amusement. At length Hatter asked him to join some croquet-players who were lacking a partner. Plainton doubtfully consented. His partner happened to be Miss Kate Templeton, who lived at the old Manor House, and of whose family the curate and his sister had seen a good deal. The lady on the opposite side was a Miss Domville, a notorious flirt, who, as the game advanced, fairly lost her temper, and began to play spitefully and fiercely.

Plainton could not but remark the quiet

amiability with which Miss Templeton bore the ill-concealed rudeness of her adversary, but he was not sorry when the game was concluded. Miss Domville's party won it, and her gleam of satisfied hate, and Miss Templeton's quiet, kindly smile, did not escape his observant eye. He entered into conversation with his partner, and asked after the members of her family.

They were soon joined by Miss Templeton's sister Ethel, a bright-eyed child of fourteen, with an abundance of chestnut-coloured hair floating down over her shoulders. Plainton looked at them with unaffected admiration. The elder sister had black hair, large, dreamy eyes, and a rich, deep damask mingled with the lily of her cheek. But what had especially struck Plainton the first time he saw her, was the pure, spiritual aspect of her face. Its owner ever seemed to be in close communion with the unseen world. When the features were in repose, as she stood apart from her companions, Plainton could well imagine that she was holding converse with the angels.

Our readers may smile, perhaps, at the curate's fanciful notions ; they may exclaim that he was a weak-pated, soft-hearted fellow. It may be so. Yet we think they will do well to reserve judgment, and wait till they have seen him in other circumstances. It is to be borne in mind that he had come from a curacy in the east end of London, where he had worked for five years amidst a dense population of poor, wretchedly-clad, ill-fed people. Absorbed in missionary enterprise, he had scarcely been out of his parish except when urgent business called him. He had had little recreation there, and no social relaxation whatever.

He felt now the contrast strongly. In talking with these two innocent simple girls he was rested and refreshed. They appeared to his weary spirit like two lovely spring flowers, formed to be admired and loved. They were both very pretty, and dressed richly but in perfect taste. They satisfied his feeling for the Beautiful, and outwardly seemed the embodiment of the Good.

Their pleasant conversation was interrupted by a loud squall from the centre of
the lawn. On looking round, Plainton saw
Hetty struggling in the hands of her mother,
and grasping at the same time a croquet
mallet as long as herself.

On inquiry, the curate found that Hetty
had been amusing herself by knocking away
the balls as soon as the players had put them
in position, but not finding this amusement
sufficiently exhilarating, had proceeded to
pluck up the hoops and throw them into the
flower-beds. As the players were somewhat
disconcerted by this pleasing attention on the
part of the Vicar's child, Mrs. Hatter had at
length come to the rescue. However, on
promising to be good, Hetty was allowed to
be at large again. Plainton watched her
movements with considerable amusement.
At first she was tolerably quiet, and only
occasionally kicked a ball out of its place ;
but by degrees she grew bolder, and began to
practise on the hoops again.

It happened that young Mr. Snobbie, who

was a great exquisite, came near the place where Hetty was standing, in order to execute a very difficult long-shot. Having measured the distance with his eye, he stood for a second or two beside his ball and carefully balanced his mallet for the stroke. Whereupon Hetty, with great suddenness and skill, lifted her mallet, and brought it down with all her little might upon his beautiful shiny hat, and very cleverly bonneted him, to the intense delight of his companions.

'You little cuss!' muttered Snobbie, re-adjusting his crushed head-covering; but observing that Mrs. Hatter had hastened to the scene, and was concerned to know if he were injured, he gracefully bowed, and with a sweet smile replied :

'Not—ah—in the least—ah—thanks. Pleasant little child—so very—ah—amusing —ah—' and proceeded with his game, as if he were rather flattered than otherwise by Hetty's kind attention. The latter, kicking and screaming, was carried indoors by Mrs. Hatter and one of the maids. Not long

afterwards, Plainton saw her at the drawing-
room window, emptying half-a-glass of claret
on the lavender silk dress of Miss Corbyn, one
of the district visitors, who was sitting under-
neath, but was wholly unconscious of what
was going on, so wrapt was she in conversation with Mrs. Grimm, on the merits of the
Vicar and his family.

' What a charming, sweet-tempered child !'
she exclaimed, with a toss of her head, and uplifted hands.

' Yes,' replied Mrs. Grimm, with a meaning look ; ' so like her dear papa !'

A little later on Plainton understood this
enigmatical allusion to the Vicar.

Presently Mrs. Chubb, advancing to the
curate with a pleasant smile, said :

' Mr. Plainton, I must introduce you to my
husband. He was in Scotland fishing, you
know, when you called.'

Plainton accordingly followed Mrs. Chubb
to the other end of the lawn, where he was
duly introduced to Mr. Chubb and his friend
Mr. John Bridge. Mr. Chubb was a wealthy

sporting character, and joint editor of *The Country Gentleman,* a high-class sporting periodical.

The Chubbs were, on the whole, much liked in the parish, although not visited by the exclusive aristocracy of Pollington. They were kindly, genial, and, it must be added, even jovial. They were not what would be termed strict-living people, though they came pretty regularly to church, especially when there was any illness in the family, or when Mr. Chubb was anticipating an attack of the gout. Being strong Evangelicals and staunch Protestants, they never subscribed to the offertory, because, as Mrs. Chubb observed :

' I do not like the chink of money in church. It sounds so very out of place—so very demoralising.'

Besides, it was collected in bags, which old Chubb said was ' a mark of the beast, and the beginning of Papistical corruption.'

For a similar reason they objected to turn to the east during the Creed ; and to mark the soundness of their reformed principles, the whole family—father, mother, three sons, and four daughters—used regularly, with great precision, to face due west, as soon as the curate began, ' I believe,' etc.

This was at first very embarrassing to Plainton, for the reading-desk was just below their two pews, and as he turned round to face east, he was punctually met by the scrutinising gaze of the eighteen bright eyes (and they were very bright) belonging to the Chubbs. We feel bound to say here, that if Plainton occasionally faltered in his recitation of the articles of the Belief, or transposed or omitted a clause, it was not owing, as some have asserted, to his weakness of faith in any single article, but was rather due to the bewildering influence exercised by the opposite phalanx of calm, unmoved optical organs of the nine Chubbs.

On the festivals on which the Athanasian Creed was appointed to be used, the Chubb family remained seated whilst it was said, as Mr. Chubb emphatically observed there was 'too much hell-fire and damnation in it' to suit his stomach.

John Bridge—the usual prefix was always dispensed with by his friends in speaking of him—was the occasional companion of Chubb in his fishing expeditions. The two men had little else in common. John Bridge, honest John Bridge, as Plainton loved to call him, was the principal of a large iron and steel foundry. He was a short, thick-set man, with a determined face, and two large, luminous black eyes, which glowed like live coals as he grew warm on any subject which moved his feelings.

Plainton and he liked one another from the beginning, perhaps it was because they were both frank and honest men. It was true John Bridge was a strong Evangelical, whilst Plainton's leanings were in an opposite direction. But he had a warm corner in his heart for the old-fashioned Low-Church party amongst which in early life his lot had been cast, and with whose loving work he deeply sympathised. As he observed to Margaret :

' If all Evangelicals were like John Bridge, it would be a good thing for the Church. For there would certainly be no " Church Persecution Company " to harry to death men who obey the rubrics.'

Honest John Bridge ! How often in after years did Plainton remember thy frank, earnest face, and invoke a blessing on the head of the man who could dare to be true as steel to his friend to the last ! But we must not anticipate.

When Plainton had spoken a few words to most of those present in the garden, he walked across the grounds to seek his sister. He saw her at last, in a remote corner, with the Langleys. As he made his way towards her he had to pass a thick-set shrubbery. As he approached it he could hear voices on the other side, although he could not see the owners of them. He recognised the tones of Mr. Chubb and John Bridge, and unintentionally heard the following fragment of their conversation before he was again out of hearing :

'It's a pity he does not dine out a little more. If he had more flesh on his bones he would be able to take life a little more easily, and wouldn't pitch into his congregation so much.'

'Oh, scissors! that be hanged!' emphatically replied the voice of John Bridge; 'he has the right metal in him. He believes what he says, and speaks like a man.'

As the curate and his sister returned to their lodgings, the former observed:

'I am glad I lost that game, for if I had won it Miss Domville would have hated me. She would never again have listened to my preaching, and I should have had no influence for good with her whatever. I doubt if it is wise for a clergyman to join in a game of croquet.'

'Why not?' returned Margaret. 'Clergymen have bodies, and must have recreation as well as other men. With your heavy brain-work, day after day, you need some such light relaxation. Solitary walks will not do you much good; and, besides, mixing socially

with your people will give you a far greater
insight into their characters than you would
get by merely formal intercourse, as you see
by what you have learnt of Miss Domville's.'

'Ah! what a dreadful temper she has! I
must certainly preach on ill-temper and
brotherly love. But do you think an apostle
would have played croquet?'

'Why should he not? I can well imagine
St. Paul joining in that or any other innocent
game, if he thought it would give pleasure to
others.'

CHAPTER IV.

MRS. CHINE.

MARGARET's prophecy recorded at the beginning of Chapter II. was destined to be speedily fulfilled. About a fortnight after their arrival Mrs. Chine called. She was a buxom-looking widow of fifty, and would have had an altogether attractive face, if it had not been for her coarse, vulgar mouth, and her small, deceitful-looking eyes. Her dress was, at first sight, bewildering. She wore a green rep, and an Indian shawl wrought in divers colours. Her bonnet was trimmed with blue, and surmounted by three tulips of extraordinary size and beauty, which nodded and waved from side to side as she talked. Her large, fat hands were enveloped in buff-coloured gauntlet gloves.

She did not stay long the first time she called, but in the following week she came again soon after breakfast. As soon as she caught sight of Margaret she exclaimed :

'Ah, my dear, how do you do ? And how is your dear brother ?'

Not waiting for an answer, she forthwith put her arms round Margaret's neck, and kissed her on both cheeks. Miss Plainton's breath was quite taken away, not only by being violently squeezed against Mrs. Chine's ample bosom, but by the novelty of the situation.

Mrs. Chine then proceeded to give Margaret a minute and faithful account of herself, beginning from the moment when she was brought into the world ; which momentous event was only safely accomplished by the aid of five doctors, as she solemnly assured Miss Plainton. Her infancy was a succession of miracles ; her youth was passed in rejecting the offers of various anxious suitors; but at last she married in order to be a missionary to her husband. He died of brain fever. After two years spent in unmitigated sorrow, she consented to become the wife of old Mr. Chine, because he had no one to take care of him, and was very fond of veal and ham pies, which he said no one could make like she could.

'And, my dear,' suddenly breaking off from her narrative to open a small basket she had brought, 'I hope you will not be offended, but I have brought one of my veal and ham pies for your dear brother. I have been thinking all the week how he is pouring out his brains all over his paper in his study for our good, and he ought to have something, however trifling, in return.'

Margaret was embarrassed. She did not like to hurt the good woman's feelings by rejecting her present, but she felt that something would have to be done about it in the future.

In spite of Margaret's gentle remonstrances and delicate hints, Mrs. Chine gave all the particulars of her married life with Mr. Chine, and wept copiously as she recounted the sad details of his sudden decease while swallowing some pastry.

Margaret fully expected that having killed off her second husband, she would now take her *own* departure. But not so. Mrs. Chine had many interesting particulars to give respecting the parishioners, which she insisted on believing would be useful to her hostess and her 'dear brother.' This was too much for poor Margaret, who exclaimed :

'But I do not like to talk or hear about my neighbours. People who talk much about their neighbours are generally uncharitable, and do not adhere strictly to the truth.'

This was pretty plain speaking, but Mrs. Chine replied, with a winning smile :

'Ah! my dear, how good of you! Just like your dear brother. But you are too innocent, my dear. You don't know what you will have to encounter in this dreadful place.'

Margaret was in despair, and thought she had better let her visitor finish her story, and

make the best of it ; but she soon repented
of her courtesy. Mrs. Chine had not a good
word for anybody—not even for the Vicar,
whose especial favourite she was supposed to
be.

At length Margaret felt that a stop must
be put to it, and interrupting her visitor just
as she was beginning to give the private history of Miss Piggott, who visited in the next
district, and was a rival in the Vicar's affec-
tions, she said firmly :

' Mrs. Chine, if you do not stop your in-
famous scandal, you shall never enter this
house again !'

The next moment she regretted her rash-
ness, for she thought : ' There ! I have made
a relentless enemy for poor Pawley, and I
am sure he has enough to think of just
now.'

Margaret had but a faint notion of the re-
sources of her visitor. Mrs. Chine stopped
her foolish talking instantly, and coming over
to Margaret affectionately embraced her, and
said :

'Ah! my dear, if all the world were like you, we shouldn't want any sermons.'

She then took her leave.

At luncheon, Margaret gave her brother an account of the interview. He thought very seriously of it, and forthwith made a note to preach a course of sermons during Lent on Gossip, Scandal, Busybodies, and Idlers. He was as good as his word.

Mrs. Chine continued to call about three times a week, but was more careful in her conversation, and as Margaret received her with marked coldness, did not stay so long. Every week, however, she sent presents of pies, or tarts, or poultry, or cough mixtures and embrocations, until Margaret felt that it must not be allowed 'to go on. Plainton remonstrated with his sister on this view. He said it would be so cruel to hurt Mrs. Chine's kindly feelings by refusing her little offerings.

'But, Pawley, I do not see any other way of stopping her scandalous tongue. If we accept her presents she immediately presumes on it, and expects to come and waste two or three mornings a week in abusing her neighbours.

'Well,' said he, smiling, 'I quite believe it takes a woman to settle a woman. So I will leave you to enjoy the task.'

The next time that Mrs. Chine called after this conversation, Margaret received her in her usual manner, and plunged at once *in medias res.* She told her visitor that they could not receive any more presents. Mrs. Chine burst into tears.

'I felt how it would be,' she sobbed, 'when I sent that pie last week—' here for some seconds she was unable to proceed. 'I ought to have kept to the veal and ham, and not tried beefsteak ! I could see from your brother's face in the pulpit that it did not agree with him. And when he spoke so earnestly of disappointment and trial, I held my head down in the pew, for I knew what he was referring to !'

Margaret for some time looked helplessly on. What was to be done to make this

woman understand that her conduct was offensive, and that Plainton and herself must
preserve their independence, if they were to
do any good in the place ?

When Mrs. Chine's agitation had in some
degree subsided, Margaret tried to make the
matter plain to her, but it is doubtful if her
visitor gained more than a glimmering of her
meaning.   However, as Margaret treated her
very tenderly, they parted on excellent
terms.

CHAPTER V.

THE TEMPLETONS.

PLAINTON's work for the pulpit, his systematic visitation of the poor, and the occasional help he afforded Mr. Hatter in his literary labours, left him but little time for recreation. Occasionally he found it absolutely necessary to desist from writing in his study, and to betake himself to the fields, because, as he observed to Margaret, his 'brain wouldn't go.'

Especially on Mondays was he exhausted, and really unfit for any mental labour whatever. He would come down to breakfast with pale, worn face, and say :

4—2

LIBRARY
UNIVERSITY OF ILLINOIS

'There's a deficiency of grey matter in the brain this morning, Margaret, due, I suppose, to the two sermons and children's service yesterday. I must get into the open air as soon as I can.'

It was but a short walk to the grounds attached to the old Manor House, the residence of the Templetons. Here he could rest unmolested under the large, spreading trees, watch the floating clouds, or listen to the song of thrush and blackbird, and later in the evening hear the plaintive lullaby of the nightingale.

Nearer the house was a high wall which enclosed the extensive lawn and flower-garden in which it was situated. There was a gate in this wall which led into the outer grounds, where Plainton usually sought rest and air. Frequently from this gate little Ethel and her younger sister Maud would come bounding towards him. The latter would seat herself at his feet, the former would take up her place by his side. He would hold a hand of Maud in one of his,

and with the other he would play with the
flowing hair of Ethel.

Oh! those happy hours, how soon have ye
fled! Much has been said of the golden
hours of childhood and youth. Plainton had
had his share of them. His solitary com-
munings with nature in boyhood were remembered with fond delight. How often
had he risen at daybreak, and gone forth to
smell the fields, to pluck the wild flowers of
the wood, and to salute the rising sun, which,
more in earnest than in jest, he called his
' brother!' These were golden hours.

But in the hours he spent by the old
Manor House, there was added a deeper joy.
Arduous toil in a densely crowded and poor
district, as well as his work at Pollington,
had tried his strength and spirit to the utter-
most. Continual contact with sin, poverty,
and unbelief had wearied him. The com-
panionship of his young friends, so innocent
even of the existence of evil, helped to restore
his elasticity of mind, and to strengthen his
burdened heart.

It is a trite saying that nature looks more beautiful in the presence of those we love. Plainton realised the truthfulness of the remark. The sun seemed to shine more brightly, the birds to sing more sweetly, the flowers to dress themselves in more lovely hues, and the river to flow on more joyously, if the children were with him.

Occasionally, as a great treat, he would put up a few sandwiches and a flask of claret, and take Ethel and Maud to Brackley Park, a good three miles' walk. There they would choose out the most sequestered spot, and, sitting down under some spreading oak, would enjoy to their hearts' content the beautiful scenery presented to them on every side.

What allegories, tales, and jokes he used to tell them! With what rippling laughter did they listen to him! Then, as the sun was beginning to hasten to the crimson west, they would seek their way back by the river to the old Manor House. There they would find a dainty repast awaiting their arrival in the schoolroom, which looked out on one end

of the lawn. Plainton would sit with his
face to the window, so as to behold the green,
well-trimmed grass, the rich flower-beds, and
the bending trees, with their grotesque and
sombre shadows.

Maud would take her place beside him,
while Ethel, assuming with some consequence
the dignity of the matron, would plant herself at the head of the table, which the generous hand and skilful taste of Kate had
already adorned with sweet-smelling flowers.

What delicious tea they sipped! What
sweet bread and butter they ate!—a tempting
meal, enjoyed with innocent mirth and childlike glee. When the hour was come for
Plainton to depart, Ethel would see him out
of the hall-door, and laughingly kiss her hand
to him as he passed through the large iron
gates—a man refreshed and strengthened for
another week's arduous toil.

CHAPTER VI.

POLLINGTON COTTAGE GARDEN FLOWER-SHOW.

ONE day in June, Plainton went to the Vicarage to arrange the details of the annual Cottage Garden Flower-Show, which was shortly to be held. As he was passing the Vicarage, he suddenly heard a loud crash of glass, and immediately afterwards received a severe blow on the side of the head from a heavy missile, which sent his hat flying to the other side of the road. As he stooped to pick up his hat, he saw that the missile was none other than Hetty's little dog, which was lying in the road in a sort of convulsive fit.

He took up the dog, and then looked round at the window. Hetty was standing looking through the hole with a pleased and defiant air. As he entered the hall Mrs. Hatter met him.

'Dear me!' said she, 'that tiresome child has broken one of the dining-room windows.'

'I hope she has not hurt the dog,' said the curate, as he entered the drawing-room, and placed Spot upon the table.

'She wanted him to draw her waggon, with the doll's house on the top of it; but the dog wouldn't or couldn't, and, before I could stop her, she had taken him up and thrown him through the window. I do not know what papa will say. It is really very tiresome.'

'I think the dog wants looking to,' said Plainton, glancing at Spot, who was kicking faintly amongst the books.

'Oh! I wish the poor thing was dead and out of his misery, for he leads a wretched life. Last week we were obliged to have one of his eyes removed, Hetty had injured it so. I gave him a little piece of pie-crust before Hetty was served, when she caught hold of his head and beat it most unmercifully with a dinner-fork. The left eye suffered most, and was so disfigured and damaged that it had to come out.'

' How very shocking !' said Plainton, wiping the mud off his hat.

' It is only when she is put out that she is so violent, otherwise she is amiable enough. I'll tell Mr. Hatter you are here.'

Mrs. Hatter disappeared to find the Vicar, taking the dog with her.

Hetty stood looking up into the curate's face with an innocent, cheerful smile. He looked at her sternly as he said :

' If you belonged to me, Hetty, I would cure you of your wicked behaviour. You are a shocking child !'

He wondered whether she would kick or throw something at him. The child was evidently struck with a style of address to which she was wholly unaccustomed ; for visitors, though dreading to be in the same room with her, always praised and petted her.

Hetty put her hand on his knee, looked wonderingly into his face, and remarked :

' You are a very funny man.'

' You wouldn't find me funny if you were my child.'

' Ha ! ha !' said Hetty, apparently regarding this as a good joke ; ' how you talk. I don't think you could do much. Look at my map ! I draw'd it all myself.'

She placed on the curate's knees a very original outline of the country. In order that there might be no mistake as to which was sea and which dry land, the former was studded with sketches of various sea-monsters, and the latter with horses and dogs in an elementary stage of construction.

' I aspose you'll find fault with that next, as you are so quarrelsome.'

She left him and ran towards the door. It opened, and Mr. Hatter entered.

' Look ! papa, at my map !'

The Vicar was seemingly ignorant of Plainton's arrival, and as he was sitting near the window in a corner, the curtains almost entirely hid him from view. Hatter was so absorbed with the child that he did not see the curate.

'Oh! my darling, how beautiful!' he exclaimed, in a full, affectionate voice, quite different from his usual hesitating tone.

Plainton was amazed beyond measure at the complete change wrought in the man's whole demeanour as he took Hetty in his arms. The hard, grasping lines disappeared from the face ; the cold, suspicious glitter of the eye gave place to an almost passionate look of love as he pressed his child to his breast. The child put her hand into his grey beard, and nestling her little face into his neck, said softly :

'Papa, dear.'

'Yes, darling.'

'I do love you so much.'

Her father smiled and pressed her closer to himself.

'You *are* a good papa.'

'Am I, darling?' he said, almost plaintively, and his eyes filled with tears.

Here Plainton thought it better to make a movement, as he felt this scene was not intended for him. It had occupied but a few seconds, and he had been too rapt with astonishment to move before.

The Vicar looked quickly over to the curate, and instantly put the child down.

'Oh !—eh—eh—I forgot you were waiting. Eh—eh—come this way.'

He made no remark about the broken window, and as they were now in the drawing-room perhaps he did not know of it. Plainton followed him into the study, and glanced at his face as he turned round to close the door. The kindly look had fled, it seemed harder and more calculating than ever. His complexion had turned to a pale, greenish hue, whilst his eye glistened with its wonted uncanny light.

He informed his curate that when he first came to the parish it was in a terrible state of anarchy; class divided against class, the poor hating the rich, the rich neglecting the poor. Further, the grossest immorality,

drunkenness, and improvidence prevailed
amongst the latter class.

'But now all this is changed,' he continued ;
'very much for the better—and—eh—eh—I
attribute it chiefly to my establishing an
annual Cottage Garden Flower-Show.'

Plainton, remembering his present experience of the parish, wondered what it could
have been in those bygone days referred to
by the Vicar.

'Now the labourer, when he has ended his
day's toil, instead of spending his evening in
the tavern, goes home to—eh—eh—his garden.
He tends his flowers, or waters his cabbages
and potatoes. His mind is enlarged, his
morals are cultivated; he refrains from what
was his nightly amusement of beating his
wife ; he clothes his children, and sends them
to school ; he saves money, and puts it in the
Post Office Savings' Bank. This is all due to
the—eh—eh—establishment of the Cottage
Garden Flower-Show.

'But not only so. This annual gathering
brings all classes together. The peer rubs

shoulders with the peasant; the titled lady
with the humble but virtuous vendor of
watercresses, and the worship of caste is fast
dying out in consequence. The attendance at
church is largely increased, and many who
were dissenters have returned to the church
of their forefathers, through the indirect influence of this annual festive gathering.'

This picture of almost millennial happiness
delighted and perplexed Plainton. He would
have given his right hand to see such a
desirable state of society brought about in
Pollington, but he could not but feel that the
Vicar was a little too imaginative. Mr.
Hatter had caught and interpreted the look
on his face, and in answer to it observed:

'Eh—eh—of course it has not had quite
sufficient time to work the desired effect in
every individual, but it is fast advancing
towards that end every year.'

The great day arrived. Mr. Chubb kindly
lent his field for the display. It was a great
show. The place was crowded. The judges,
who were florists and nurserymen of the

neighbourhood, met early in the morning and assigned the prizes.

As Plainton was going home to his luncheon, he saw a great crowd outside the grounds, and inquired what was the matter of a bystander.

'Oh! it is only Ned Clancy and Dick Stumper settling the prize. It was given to Clancy for carrots and potatoes, but Stumper says his are the best. As they were both " a little on " the quarrel has got to blows, but I don't think Stumper has the weight for it.'

With some little difficulty the men were separated, sharing a broken nose and black eye between them. Then the two combatants with their respective followings adjourned to the Pig and Whistle for refreshments.

Returning to the enclosure early in the afternoon, the curate saw old Mr. Broadbeam standing, with his hands in his pockets, at his garden-gate.

Broadbeam was the treasurer of the Flower-Show Society. He had been a wholesale tradesman in Manchester, where every

morning he had been accustomed to stand at
his shop-door for half an hour to get an
appetite for breakfast. His circumstances
were changed, but the habit remained and
had grown. Several half-hours during the
day, now he had no customers to serve, were
spent at his door. He had amassed an immense fortune, and was a very useful public
man, holding several local offices beside that
of county magistrate.

As Plainton came up he could see he was
in a furious rage.

' Did you ever know anything so scan-
dalously unfair ?' he blurted out. ' There's
old Beets, who occasionally does a day's work
for me, and grows the best geraniums in the
place, has not got even a " mention " at the
show. There is no doubt that MacPhunny
has influenced the judges against him. I
shall resign if the committee don't take the
matter up.'

, The curate felt very much cast down by
these two instances of the moral effect of the
flower-show, and after a few more words with

the irate treasurer, he passed on and entered the grounds.

A very superior brass band had been hired from Tonford. Each man was to receive his dinner, a gallon of beer, and five shillings; and was to play at intervals through the day.

The musicians had performed very fairly during the morning, but after dinner it was found very difficult to get the men together again. When at length they were mustered, at least half of them were visibly suffering from the effects of the allotted gallon apiece, and the big drum was missing altogether. He was at last discovered fast asleep on the floor of the tent, but as he was unable to stand, it was thought advisable to dispense with the big drum for the rest of the day.

After a great deal of coaxing and preliminary adjustment, the band managed to strike up a set of quadrilles. The conductor with his bâton looked imposing; but the men under his command had suffered a good deal on previous occasions from his tyranny, and feeling, after dinner, tolerably independent, as if by tacit consent altogether ignored his beating. In fact each man, being a freeborn Briton, exercised his right to take his own time, and in some instances to extemporise his own music. The more furiously the irate conductor protested, shouted, and gesticulated, the more vigorously did they blow their own time and their own music.

The effect may be imagined. Not since music has been known to man as the soother of his sufferings and the interpreter of his joys, has there been heard such a horrible screeching discord of sounds. People stopped in their promenade to ask what was the matter, and looked from one to another with agonised countenances. Several members of the committee were appealed to, and these gentlemen, most of whom had been having a little luncheon in an adjoining tent, rushed towards the heated musicians.

Broadbeam and Chubb were the first to arrive.

'Stop that infernal row, you rascally set of scoundrels!' cried the former; while the latter, preferring deeds to words, collared the half-tipsy bassoon. The latter held on to his instrument, so did Mr. Chubb. Bassoon shouted to a friend for help, who immediately joined issue with the intruder; and the next moment all three were rolling on the ground, still holding on manfully to the instrument.

Broadbeam was not received with any greater degree of politeness than was his unfortunate brother committee-man. The conductor resented the remarks of the treasurer, as soon as he understood what they were, and declared they were all as good as he, and some perhaps a little better. Broadbeam, shaking his stick at him, told him he was a scurrilous cur. The sentence was scarcely out of his mouth, when his hat was knocked over his eyes.

Others of the committee went to the rescue of their leaders, and in a few moments there was a scene of indescribable confusion. Forms, chairs, and stands were broken, instruments smashed, coats torn, and several bodies bruised. The bandsmen, half-stupefied with drink and blowing combined, laid about them with anything that came to hand, while the conductor, irritated alike by friend and foe, seizing half of a music-stand, dealt vigorous blows with equal impartiality upon his unlucky musicians and those who attacked them.

When at length, by the aid of the police something like order was restored, the harmonious musicians were marched out of the enclosure with forlorn-looking instruments and in disreputable attire, Broadbeam hospitably assuring them, as they went along, that he would have the whole infernal lot of them up before him next week, and give them a month apiece.

Later in the evening the prizes were distributed by Lady Carmine. As Plainton made his way towards the platform, he fell in with Kate Templeton and her sisters.

' Is it not a shame, Mr. Plainton ?' said she indignantly ; ' Mr. Chubb's sister-in-law from Yorkshire, who was never in the place till yesterday, and is going away again to-

morrow, is to receive the prize for table deco-
ration. I always understood that these prizes
were for residents; it says so on the bill.'

Their conversation was interrupted by the
stentorian voice of Dr. Rowland Jolly an-
nouncing the names of the winners of prizes.
He began with the ladies. No one responded
to the first name, nor yet to the second, nor
to the third; and Dr. Jolly got to the end of
the ladies' list without a single resident in
Pollington appearing.

It is easily explained. Lady Carmine was
not a favourite in the neighbourhood. It was
felt that she had neglected Pollington; for all
her visitors came from London, and no one in
the place, except Hatter, had been known to
be within her walls as a guest. When it was
understood that she would distribute the
prizes, the ladies determined not to appear,
and they kept their word.

There was, however, one lady prize-winner
from the neighbouring district of St. Patrick's,
who responded to her name; but she would
not have come up had it not been for the

earnest entreaties of her Vicar, the Rev. Blather Sope, a noted member of the Church Persecution Society, who was anxious to get an introduction to Lady Carmine's garden-parties. He had only lately taken possession of St. Patrick's. He had been a student of St. Magnus' Theological College, but having failed three times to pass the final examination, the authorities at last granted to his tears what they refused to his Greek. He was, however, a shrewd, worldly man, with a great gift of words. By the continual asking of his friends, some of whom were titled nobodies, he obtained from the archbishop a B.D. degree, which excited the mirth of the whole Rural Deanery ; and Dr. Blather Sope, as he was termed by courtesy, being regarded as the symbol of the archbishop's theological attainments, was generally spoken of as ' Archbishop's Theology.'

The prizes assigned to the cottagers were next distributed, to the delight of the recipients and the envious disappointment of the unsuccessful candidates.

As Lady Carmine left the ground, she was heard to say, that she would never again take part in any public proceeding affecting the Pollingtonians.

Plainton returned home with a heavy heart. As he passed though the streets he noticed that the public-houses were crowded with drunken men and women, and the cursing and swearing about the various incidents of the day thrilled him with horror. He retired to rest deeply impressed with the moral effects wrought by the Pollington annual Cottage Garden Flower-Show.

CHAPTER VII.

DARGAL LODGE.

ONE evening in the summer, Plainton and his sister went to the Broughams, who lived in the Grove, to have a little music. The curate had a very fair tenor voice, and used to sing some Italian and English songs.

On this particular evening the Broughams were not alone. A married sister was staying with them, and a Miss Mona Melody, who lived at Dargal Lodge, near Tonford, the adjoining village to Pollington, was also there. The Plaintons had never met her before. She was a striking-looking girl, noble in bearing, tall, and with prominent but remarkably handsome features. She had a well-developed figure, rather a full throat, and a skin of exquisite whiteness and purity. Her forehead was broad, her hair blue-black, and her eyes dark, large, and fringed with long black eyelashes. Her complexion was very pale, almost too much so to be pleasing; and occasionally a half-melancholy smile settled on her face. She was dressed with great simplicity, but in extremely good taste.

When she was introduced to the Plaintons she bowed slightly, but did not speak, though her lips moved. She seemed to be very reserved, if she were not silent from mere pride. After Plainton had sung 'Adelaide' and 'Agathe,' Miss Brougham asked Miss Melody to sing an Irish ballad. She rose from her seat without speaking, and seated herself at the piano, when she sang, 'Oh! breathe not his name!' There was something painfully intense in the feeling which she threw into the song. It was not that she sang it better than Plainton had ever heard it sung before, but there was a peculiar quality in her voice, which gave an almost unearthly tone to her notes.

When she had finished, the curate offered her a chair, and in all sincerity thanked her for her song.

' Do you like the Irish ballads ?' she asked.

' Yes, when properly sung.'

' Perhaps you have Irish friends ?'

' One or two. In fact, I believe there is some Irish blood in my veins, but not much.'

' I thought there was when you came into the room ; but I could not detect the slightest accent in your enunciation.'

' No,' said Plainton, laughing, ' I do not suppose you would. I was born in London, and lived there during the early years devoted to the acquisition of speech.'

' Ah ! I was educated in Dublin.'

' I presume that accounts for the just sufficient Hibernian flavour you put into the song, and without which it would be utterly insipid.'

' I see you know what Tom Moore's ballads require to sound effective.'

Thence their conversation led them to a comparison of the national melodies of the three kingdoms.

The cold dignity and reserve, which had marked her in the early part of the evening, were quite gone, and Plainton found her frank, easy, and communicative. At half-past nine Miss Melody left with her servant, when Miss Brougham informed the Plaintons, that she led a very lonely life, as her people went out but little; and that both her father and mother were of Irish extraction, the former holding, it was supposed, some Crown appointment, almost a sinecure, which brought him into intimate relations with the Earl of Castledown, and not being often seen at home.

Some weeks passed without Plainton hearing or seeing anything more of Miss Melody. On the first Sunday in the following month, Margaret said that she was at the early celebration with her brother.

Later on, when the 'Winter Evening Entertainments' began, Miss Melody and her brother appeared at the opening one. Margaret, who was sitting in the body of the room, spoke to them at the close of the entertainment. Presently her brother joined them, and walked to the corner of the road with them. In the following week, while Plainton and his sister were out, cards were left with the names of Mr., Mrs., and Miss Melody, and Mrs. Eugénie Constantine, Dargal Lodge, Tonford. The call was returned after a considerable delay, the curate and his sister being much engaged with parish work. Mrs. Melody and her daughter were at home when they went, and the visitors were received with geniality. Mrs. Melody informed them, that they seldom went anywhere except to church at Tonford, though Mona preferred to go to the service at Pollington. Occasionally during the season, Miss Melody went to a ball with Mrs. Constantine, and paid a rare visit to the Broughams, who were the only people they knew in Pollington.

As they walked home, taking the shorter road by the river, Plainton remarked what a heaviness there seemed to be about the house. Perhaps it was owing to the furniture, which was old, cumbrous, and very dark.

Shortly afterwards Arthur Melody called with an invitation to dinner, which was accepted. When they went, they were introduced to Mrs. Eugénie Constantine, a middle-aged widow with a very fair complexion. Miss Melody was dressed wholly in white, with a large gold cross suspended from her neck, and a white camellia in her dark hair. Plainton again noticed the unnatural pallor of her face, and the peculiar tone of her voice. As the evening wore on, her cheeks became slightly flushed, and the reserve and melancholy which seemed habitual to her quite passed away.

'I cannot get reconciled to that house,' said the curate, when he and his sister left at ten o'clock. 'It seems so dark and heavy. The very atmosphere of the place feels laden with mystery. I felt my heart sink within

me as we entered. I should scarcely have
been startled to hear the cry of the Banshee.
Do you know anything about the family
more than the Broughams have said?'

'Not much. Mrs. Chubb said the other
day that she had seen Mr. Melody at the
Norfolk Hotel, Brighton, with Lord Castledown, and that there were various unpleasant
rumours afloat about his gambling pro-
pensities.'

'Who is Mrs. Eugénie Constantine?'

'The bosom friend of Mrs. Melody. She
taught her daughter to sing and play the harp.'

'I don't like her manner.'

'You forget that she is of Spanish origin,
and would hardly have an English manner.'

'Miss Melody seems to me quite out of
place there. That girl ought to see more
people.'

'I think so too,' said Margaret, in a thought-
ful tone. 'I should not go there very often
if I were you.'

'I do not intend. The place gives me a
sort of nightmare. I wish——'

'Look at that man!' whispered Margaret, suddenly laying her hand on her brother's arm.

They had now come to the gate of their lodgings; as he opened the door, Plainton turned, and saw a man on the opposite side walking slowly by. He had on a long, dark overcoat, a wide-awake hat, and a muffler round his throat.

'I don't see anything particular about him,' said the curate.

'He has been close behind us all the way from Dargal Lodge.'

'What of that? It is a public road.'

'Yes, I know,' said his sister, as they sat down to some cocoa; 'but, Pawley, I cannot help thinking that we have been followed the last two or three times that we have been out.'

'Oh! what nonsense, Margaret! Something has disagreed with you. Pray do not get such fancies into your head.'

Plainton had placed himself with his back to the window which faced the Green, while

Margaret sat opposite to it. Suddenly she stopped in her eating, and exclaimed in a startled voice, pointing to the window :

'Look, Pawley !'

He turned round, but saw nothing.

'What was it ?'

'A man's white face peering in between the blind and the side of the window.'

Her brother rushed to the door, and into the street. No one was to be seen. He looked up the little lane by the side of the house, but all was quiet there. His sister must have been mistaken. He returned, and said :

'Margaret, your nerves are quite unstrung. I am sure you are suffering from indigestion. Or else,' he added, laughing, 'the banshee they keep at Dargal Lodge has uttered a spell over you. Come, get to bed and sleep it off.'

They went upstairs. Plainton stayed in his sister's room a considerable time, smoking a pipe and telling one or two amusing stories, until he thought she was quite calm. Then he went to his own room.

Although he had made light of the matter
to Margaret, he felt that something was amiss.
She had been noted from a child for having
an observant and remarkably accurate eye.
But who should follow them ?   And for what
purpose should they be watched ?   He could
make nothing of it.

In his devotions that night, Plainton in-
serted the collect containing the petition :
' Keep us both outwardly in our bodies, and
inwardly in our souls.'   Then lying down
under the shadow of the Almighty wings, he
slept peacefully till morning.

Margaret was down before him, an unusual
thing.

' Well, Margaret,' he said cheerfully, as he
kissed his sister, ' where is your banshee ?'

Margaret, pointing to the garden-plot in
front of the house, replied, ' There !'

Her brother looked through the window,
and saw two or three deep marks in the earth,
apparently made by a long, narrow boot.

' It might have been a drunken man,' sug-
gested Plainton.

'It might. If so, it was an odd coincidence.'

He said no more, but determined to keep
a sharp look-out for anything more of the
kind. Margaret knew he would do this, if he
could once be got to believe as she did about
it, and she was quite willing to rely on his
courage and judgment.

CHAPTER VIII.

THE SAYINGS AND DOINGS OF MRS. CHINE.

AFTER the rebuff recorded in Chapter IV., Mrs. Chine did not come near the Plaintons for a fortnight. Margaret saw her pass the house nearly every day about luncheon-time, but she did not come up to the door. At length she called, and made inquiries of Mrs. Evans, but did not attempt to come in.

This went on for another week. On the following Monday, when Plainton had returned from a long walk in Brackley Park, he found a box on the table, and a note addressed in Mrs. Chine's handwriting. When his sister came in from her district they opened the box, which was very carefully packed. It contained a custard and a rhubarb tart.

Margaret was extremely indignant.

'They shall go back at once,' she exclaimed.

'You had better read the note first.'

It was as follows :

'3 Myrtle Villas, Molton Road,
'Monday,

'MY DEAR MISS PLAINTON,

'It is so long since I had the oppotunety of speaking to you and your dear Brother, that I hope you will excuse the liberty I take in writing to you with Ink and paper.

'Your dear Brother looked So ill on Sunday that I could not help, speaking about it to Mrs. Chubb as we came out of church not but what, we Always speak most respectful of you my dear—for I will never allow otherways though Miss Piggott do try to get a word in sumtimes. and Mrs. Chubb said that Mr. Chubb said that your dear Brother Did not Get half Enough to eat. but Mrs. Chubb said he wanted more Fat, more Fat as she

kept Riterating shaking her Head sorrow-
fully. But I said I thought the Blood was
two thin but not to contradict Mrs. Chubb
that Fat to was wanting.

'O what a Lovely Sermon—but my dear,
it would be better I think if he did not
Heave his Stommache quite so much into it
as it must effect His Head at Last. Not but.
what I always cry and sumtimes do not eat
my Dinner in consequence. And so my
Dear with your kind Permission I send by
anne a little custard for Fat according to
Mrs. Chubb's views and rubarb tart which
Chine always used to say was good for the
Blood if not eaten two much at a time as
that wold be weekening. I have been carefull
not to send any more Meat and Pooltry according to your wishes.

'With kind Love to yourself and Kindest
Regards to your dear Brother, Believe me,

'My Dear Miss Plainton,

'Your very afecte,

'SARAH ANN CHINE.

'Anne will call next week for the dishes.'

'Well, this is beyond all bearing,' said Margaret. 'What is to be done with this woman? Are we to be persecuted like this week after week? Mrs. Evans shall take them back at once.'

'Don't let us be too hasty about it, Margaret. It will bear thinking of a little. I think her attentions spring from a kindly motive.'

'But people's kindness should be tempered with discretion, and not assume so offensive a form.'

'Well, I shouldn't send them back.'

'Then I will give them to Mrs. Evans, and tell Mrs. Chine what I have done.'

This plan was adopted. When Mrs. Chine's servant came for the dishes, she received a note for her mistress from Margaret, telling her briefly how their contents had been disposed of.

Mrs. Chine evidently did not so easily get over this slight. It touched her on a very tender point. She prided herself upon her pastry, and the tart had not been even tasted by the curate or his sister.

It was fully a month before she began to recover. Then, one fine morning, soon after breakfast, she called at the curate's lodgings. She was in great trepidation when she first saw Margaret; but, as the latter received her in her usual calm manner, she quickly regained her self-possession.

Margaret did not intend to make any reference to Mrs. Chine's last present, but Mrs. Chine did not mean to let the matter rest without an explanation.

'My dear,' she began, wiping her eyes, 'you cannot think how I have grieved over your note. If you knew how night after night——'

'Mrs. Chine, the less you say on that matter the better.'

'Certainly, my dear. But I do think it was so cruel to give them away to a stranger who knows nothing about crust, and perhaps never saw a custard in her life, except on other people's tables. And you know, my dear, you said before you would not have meat or poultry, so I thought you meant you wanted pastry and custards.'

'I remember quite well what I said,' said Margaret, wearily ; 'I intimated that I would not have any eatables.'

'There, my dear,' triumphantly exclaimed Mrs. Chine ; 'I said so—no eatables—surely you don't call a custard and tart eatables ! For as Chine used to say, when you have eaten all you can, a custard takes up no room and settles itself down in the corners without giving any trouble.'

Margaret sighed in her helpless misery.

'Well, Mrs. Chine,' she said at length, 'I have some work to do, and must go. I hope you will understand in future that we do not wish you to spend your money on us in any form whatever. There are plenty of people in the district who will be grateful for your gifts if you wish to be charitable. At the same time we thank you for your kind intentions.'

'Very well, my dear,' cheerfully replied Mrs. Chine, rising. 'Won't you take these

few flowers, then, out of my garden, to put
on your brother's table ?'

'We do not object to flowers out of your
own garden,' said Margaret, smiling, 'and Mr.
Plainton will be pleased to accept of them.'

Mrs. Chine departed quite propitiated.
As she walked across the Green she met Miss
Piggott coming from the Vicarage.

'Mr. Hatter wants to see you,' said the
latter.

'I am just going to him, so you need not
trouble yourself to tell me,' replied the good
lady, sweeping majestically past her rival.

She found the Vicar in the drawing-room.

'How are you, Mrs. Chine ? How lovely
your complexion is this morning !'

'I know you don't mean it,' said she
archly, and blushing to the roots of her hair.

'Oh ! yes, I do. You have the best complexion in Pollington.'

'Some people do not think so'—looking
aggrieved.

'I am sure Mr. Plainton does, but he is
too modest to say so before your face.'

'I know his sister talks against me. All the mischief in the place comes from her.'

A yellow gleam shot out of the corner of the Vicar's eye at the mention of Miss Plainton.

'Now, Mrs. Chine, I must not listen to any scandal, but' (dropping his voice) 'if you know of a certainty anything that Miss Plainton has done or said, you may tell me in confidence, but it must not be repeated.'

'Oh! she is always poisoning the minds of people against you and Mrs. Hatter. It is perfectly awful the way she goes on. Any one would think that she was the Vicar's wife instead of being the curate's sister.'

'Well, I must not listen to any scandal, but do you know where they have been visiting lately?'

'On Monday Mr. Plainton went to Brackley Park. My Anne says she saw him coming home with two ladies, but she could not catch them up to see who they were. On Tuesday they had a beef-steak pudding for dinner. In the afternoon they were in the

district visiting, and in the evening went to
Dr. Jolly's. They went home again at ten
o'clock. On Wednesday they had chops for
dinner, and did not go out except to church.
On Thursday—let me see—oh, yes, I remember—they had stewed steak, and went
to Mrs. Langley's in the evening. They left
at half-past nine. On Friday they had dried
haddock for dinner, and did not go out, except
in the district lanes. On Saturday they had
cutlets, and made no calls. Those Templeton
girls called on Thursday—bold, brazen things
—they have not a particle of modesty, to be
calling on a single man as they do.'

'I must hear no scandal, Mrs. Chine,' said
the Vicar, who had been listening with rapt
attention to all the woman's petty details;
'but do you know how long the Templetons
stayed?'

'Quite twenty minutes by Mrs. Tobin's
clock, who lives next door.'

'Has any one else called?'

'Miss Brougham and her sister last week;
Mrs. Bridge and Mrs. Chubb yesterday.'

' You need not talk of it in the parish, but I should like to know whom they visit at Tonford, and—if—eh—they see much of the Templetons. But I must not on any account, Mrs. Chine, permit you to talk scandal. I am determined to banish all idle gossip and mischievous tale-bearing away from the place,' said the Vicar, assuming a terribly severe tone.

' Oh! you may depend on me,' replied his active detective, closing her eyes and drawing her lips tightly together.

On leaving the Vicarage she walked through the principal streets of the village, and meeting there with one or two of the Abigails belonging to families with which the curate and his sister were intimate, entered into conversation with them. As Mrs. Chine was always affable to servants, and apparently took a particular interest in their welfare, they rewarded her courtesy by supplying her with various scraps of information respecting the Plaintons, which the good woman carefully treasured up until her next visit to the Vicarage.

Next she called on the grocer and butcher who supplied the curate's humble wants. They both thought he was starving himself. Feeling that she had now satisfied her exacting conscience by her benevolent labours, she returned home, where her own servant gave her a few more interesting items, which she had extracted from the milkman, the baker, and Mrs. Tobin's little girl, who was a constant visitor in Mrs. Chine's kitchen.

About a fortnight after this interview a large hamper arrived at the curate's lodgings, with a note, which we here transcribe from the original :

'3 Myrtle Villas, Molton Road,
'Tuesday.

'MY DEAR MISS PLAINTON,

'I hope you will give me credit for not troubling you much since I last called. But my dear I allways respect your wishes for your dear Brothers sake.

'All in the parish are very sorry that he takes on so about the wickedness of the place. But my dear we ought to be thankfull there

is some sin in the world for if everybody was
good what would be the use of keeping
Christmas Day ? But we know what he says
is all for our Benifit and that we Richly Deserve it. Excuse me my dear for saying it
but I notice during the last week or two, that
your Dear Brothers' complection is enclined
to be more Yellow than it used. Mrs. Chubb
thinks its worry and the Vicar. But I say
no, it is more serious it's want of Green Meat
which, I know my dear you cannot get
Always so nice as should be at the shops.
You know you said the other day that any
thing which came out of my own Garden and
did not cost me any money you wold accept
for your Dear Brothers sake. So I have
sent a little Green Meat and Vegetables
with some Flowers. I did not Spend a far-
thing on them except Little Johnny Dicks
brought me the manyure for the Garden and
I Gave him a peny. Please tell your Dear
Brother not to worry because we are so bad,
we shall never be as good as he is and he
Ought to be Glad that he has stopt so much

of the Wicked Gosiping and Scandle—Many I can mention are Afraid to open their mouths for Fear he should put them in his Sermon. Now my dear Miss Plainton I must conclude as Anne is waiting With kindest Regards to your Dear Brother ; and Best Love to Yourself.

'From y^r afect^e

'Sarah Ann Chine.

'I will send for the Hamper. Beware of Miss P. my Dear. She's no friend to you at the Vicarage and tells everything.'

Plainton opened the hamper. The top was overspread with a quantity of cut-flowers, then came a layer of apples, followed by a deep formation of cabbages and green meat of various kinds. The lowest strata were composed of potatoes, turnips, and carrots.

A few days after this Miss Plainton met Mrs. Chine in the village. Margaret explained that the latter had misunderstood her wishes, and that if she sent anything more to the house she would never be admitted again.

'My dear,' said Mrs. Chine, aghast, 'don't shut your door against me, whatever you do. Everybody looks to me for information about your dear brother, and they will not believe a word I tell them when they see I am not admitted.'

. 'You know how to prevent it.'

'Yes, my dear, but never think of shutting your door. I need not, I am sure, remind a clergyman's sister of the blessed promise, " Knock, and it shall be opened unto you." I know you, as a lady reverend, will never go against the Bible, my dear.'

'You don't know what you are saying, you incorrigible woman,' said Margaret, with a smile.

Mrs. Chine felt that the last epithet must be very complimentary, as Margaret's stern look had vanished, and she replied, blushing :

'It is very good of you to say so, my dear, but it is not everybody who gives me so good a name. But we must bear our cross.'

'No more of that, Mrs. Chine, please.'

'Certainly not, my dear. We ought to

suffer in silence. But, my dear, it is rather hard when you and your brother go to No. 5, in my row, and do not call on me.'

'We cannot go everywhere at once.'

'No, my dear, but to pass the very door! I often see your brother go by, and it makes me feel very solemn when he comes so near. I always read the Commination Service when he makes calls in our road, and does not come to me. For there's a word there for everybody.'

CHAPTER IX.

THE CURATE-IN-CHARGE.

The Vicar was at this time in Scotland, whither he had gone at the end of July. He was to be away a month. At the end of that time he wrote to say that as he was not very well, he would be obliged to remain a week or two longer.

'When are you going to have your holiday, Pawley? I am sure you want it badly. This place is much too relaxing, and you have worked like a slave the whole time you have been here.'

'Oh! that will be all right. Hatter is sure to be generous. Besides, there's his own letter. Don't you remember, he said if there were any difficulty about it through unforeseen circumstances, he would share it with me ?'

'Yes. It appears to me the division will be something like "Heads I win, tails you lose." You are to do the work, and he is to take the holidays.'

'Come, come, we must not judge harshly. We shall see when he returns from Scotland.'

The Vicar returned at the end of September. Plainton expected to hear each day something about his holiday. A fortnight passed, when, as they were coming from church, Mr. Hatter said :

'Eh—eh—you have not said anything about a holiday. Eh—eh—I dare say you would like to go away for a change. How little do you think you could do with ? My throat is getting very troublesome again, and I must go abroad early in November. Next year I hope to give you a longer holiday. Could you manage with one Sunday ?'

Plainton was very disappointed. He was

weary and depressed with over-work. A thorough change to a bracing climate for a few weeks would have set him up again. Seeing that the Vicar had so completely ignored his own promise, he would not condescend to say anything further than—

'If you cannot spare me for a longer time, I will say no more.'

'Thank you. You will be careful not to do any duty for your friends while you are away, as that would spoil the benefit you might derive from the change.'

Plainton said nothing.

'In thirteen days,' said Hatter, magniloquently, 'you might go to Paris, or the Alps, or——'

'Yes, I might, if I had the means,' said Plainton, shortly.

'Oh! don't let that stand in the way. If you run short of money while you are away, drop me a line, and I will send a post-office order for a small amount immediately.'

'I shall not do that, I think, thank you.'

Plainton could not help remarking to Mar-

garet on this interview, that vicars very
generally seemed to forget that they once
were curates themselves.

'It is so strange that they should begrudge
a holiday to their curates. I have already
suffered from this form of selfishness. If a
holiday is at last granted through very shame,
it is often given with an ill-grace, and perhaps with an attempt to clip off a few days
either at the beginning or end on some petty
plea.'

'Well, you will know better when you are
vicar.'

'I hope so. However, it is a melancholy
satisfaction to feel that as my chances of preferment are infinitesimally small, I shall
probably escape the demoralising process
which nearly every man seems to pass through
who is transformed from a curate into a
vicar.'

It is only fair to the curate to say that
he recovered his good temper before the day
was out.

Notwithstanding the most scrupulous

economy, Plainton's expenses at Pollington, which was a very dear place to live in, had consumed the whole of his stipend, and he had, after paying his bills, but a few shillings left in his pocket. It was impossible to go away to the sea-side, so he determined to go to his home in the country, and make walking excursions in the neighbourhood.

He was quite satisfied to do this. At an early age he had been transplanted from London to a country town. This was the place of his schoolboy days. There was an air of quiet repose about it, which fitted in with the dreams of his youth. After the struggles and disappointments of early manhood, he still found it the place of his deepest rest. His mother was there, and he wished for nothing better than to be still with her, to commune with nature, and take counsel as to the future.

Soon after the curate's return from his brief holiday, the Vicar went abroad to winter in the East, and the former was left in charge. Three or four days after Mr.

Hatter's departure, Plainton received the following letter:

> 'Hôtel de Rivoli, Rue de Rivoli, Paris.
>
> 'Nov. 4, 18—.

'(*Private.*)

'MY DEAR PLAINTON,

'Letters may be sent to the above address until Saturday week, when I will give you further instructions.

'I trust you are feeling stronger than when I left. Do not attempt too much. A break-down now would be very inconvenient. The two blue pills I gave you should be taken on Monday, as that will leave you ample time to recover your strength for Sunday.

'I forgot to tell Humm not to give away meat-tickets during my absence. If any people are out of work, he might distribute amongst them a few packets of Epsom salts. For if they have nothing to do, they will probably be idling about the public-house, and a little cooling medicine will be beneficial. You will find the key of the medicine-chest in the little drawer in my study.

'Mrs. Taylor's daughter has been to the Vicarage two or three times for port wine for her mother. She will probably come to you. As the poor woman has been given up by the doctor, and cannot last long, port wine would only hasten her dissolution, and perhaps cloud her mind at the last trying moment—which is not desirable. Humm might give her a small quantity of sal volatile ; but the daughter must bring her own bottle.

'When I left Pollington, Hingston was very ill. I have no doubt you have seen him. He was formerly a publican, and amassed an immense fortune, but led a very godless life. I hope you will be able to make an impression on him, and bring him to repentance. The proof of repentance is amendment of life. He will never be able to get up again to show his amendment. The only thing he can do is to leave a large sum of money for charitable or sacred purposes—say five hundred pounds to remove the debt on the Vicarage, so as to relieve the heavy burden which will otherwise fall on my successor. Or, he might give three hundred pounds to the Vicarage, and two hundred pounds for the purchase of copies of my " *Extinct Dialects of the Zulus,*" for distribution amongst the deserving poor at Christmastime. We ought not only to feed the bodies, but to provide wholesome food for the inquiring minds of our suffering poor.

' I cannot express to you how much I value your able services. I trust you will make up your mind to settle amongst us until you receive preferment, which I have reason to believe will be offered you at no distant date. You know that I have been expecting for some time to receive the living of Cunningstone, the present rector being almost bedridden. This is in the strictest confidence. My successor at Pollington should be a man who is already acquainted with the people, and knows how to manage them. I have already talked the matter over with the bishop, and you may consider it settled.

' See what you can do with Hingston. His head is very weak at times.

'May a rich blessing attend your truly apostolical labours !

'Ever yours,

'ENOCH HATTER.

'P.S.—If anything unforeseen occurs requiring advice, send a telegram. I will bear half the expense.—E. H.'

Plainton found the work in winter very severe, both on account of the season and of the Vicar's absence. The charitable institutions were then in full action, and the curate was responsible for their funds. There was also a good deal of business to be transacted relating to Hatter's own affairs. Plainton had to open all letters for him, forward those which seemed important, and send abstracts of the contents of the others. The Vicar's literary correspondents were numerous, and every day brought letters to be acknowledged or inquiries to be answered.

The curate's chief trouble was the spiritual

condition of the parish.   He felt it was
highly unsatisfactory.   There were wanting
in the members of the congregation faith,
fervour, and reverence.   People estimated one
another almost entirely by a worldly standard.
Wealth was exalted very nearly to the position of a god, being more esteemed than
intellectual power or high morality.   The
gossip and scandal rife in the place were a
virulent disease, and he felt there could be no
growth in holiness until this dread evil had
been eliminated.

Not more than a score of the poor, of whom
there were more than a thousand, ever went to
church.   But this was in some degree due to
the fact that no adequate provision was made
for their attendance.   When Plainton first
came into the parish, he inquired of the Vicar
how many seats were free.   ' More than half,'
said Hatter.   But this half was distributed
in draughty nooks or dark corners below,
and in the west gallery where nothing could
be heard but the organ. The poor who came to
church were made to feel that they were poor.

It is true that a few seats were assigned to them near the pulpit, but these three or four seats were carefully partitioned off from the rest of the church, and those who ventured to sit in them looked like prisoners in the dock, placed there for trial. Besides their peculiar appearance, these seats were so contrived that few people constructed on the present pattern of the human race could sit in them for any length of time without intense suffering. They were extremely narrow, very close together, and backed by a high rail which came just above the shoulders of most of the sitters. The curate observed some conscientious worshippers enduring the agony it gave them after the first half hour with the fortitude of martyrs. Again and again they were compelled to rub their pained, numbed, and cramped bodies so far as they could get at themselves to do it. None of them knelt after the first attempt, for if they once got on their knees they could never get up again without help on both sides.

Some few good seats in desirable positions

had been at first free, but most of these had
been let since the advent of the present Vicar,
owing to the growth of the population.　Miss
Plainton sat in one of the unlet pews for a
short time, but by a curious coincidence that
very one was let under her, although there
were many other sittings in a similar position.

She tried a second, that was said to be let
the following week ; and so was a third, after
she had once sat in it.　Margaret then tried
a 'free' seat, but immediately received an
intimation from the polite Vicar that she must
not occupy the places reserved for our poorer
brethren.　She then inquired of the worthy
churchwarden—a good, kind-hearted fellow,
but no match for the subtle sinuosities of Mr.
Hatter—where she might sit, or if, there being
no sitting for her, she might bring her own
camp-stool.　Margaret was informed in
confidence that the Vicar had expressed his
opinion that she ought to pay for her sitting.

Both the curate and his sister considered
that this was a vicious principle which would
bear hardly on a married man with a family,

and the broad hint was not taken. She found refuge at last in one of the pews rented by good Mr. English, the head-master of the Grammar School, who kindly offered her this spare seat amongst his boys, when he heard how Margaret was wandering round the church without finding a place of rest.

In speaking of the low spiritual standard of the people of Pollington, it is to be observed that there were some who had not bowed the knee to Baal : spiritually-minded men and noble-hearted women, who hailed with joy every effort made by the curate to improve the condition of the people. It was in a great degree owing to the kindly influence exerted by these, that Plainton consented to toil on, hoping against hope to see at last some practical result of his teaching. These received him with open arms, backed up anything he started, and freely opened their purses to him for any object he desired to carry out. How often in after years did he think of the tenderness, delicacy, and generosity with which they treated him !

It happened that on the day appointed for
special intercession on behalf of Missions, the
services at Pollington church were but thinly
attended.   The curate reflected that where
there is lack of missionary enterprise there is
lack of life.   The Church has ever done most
for those outside her pale when the lamp of
love has burnt brightest in the temple of God.
He was deeply moved by this apparent indifference.

The following Sunday was the Fourth in
Advent.   Plainton preached from the words of
the Epistle—'The Lord is at hand.'   He
spoke first of the need of preparation for the
Lord's coming, and this led him to speak of
the spiritual condition of his own people.   He
gave utterance at last to the weighty thoughts
which had been so long gathering in his heart.
He spoke of his own work and responsibility ;
of the spiritual deadness surrounding them ;
of the unbelief, the sloth, the indifference of
most of them to their highest interests, their
devotion to mere worldly trifles. He described
the worldly woman, her whole energies ab-

sorbed in giving, or going to, parties—in dressing, shopping, idle visiting, and elegant trifling. He described the worldly man, devoted to money-seeking, planning and scheming to increase his comforts and luxuries, and giving no thought to the judgment to come. Then, speaking of his own isolation in the parish, he concluded in painfully earnest tones :

'I can imagine a congregation wholly asleep, lulled to deathlike slumber. I can imagine a pastor in like condition, careful to say nothing which shall disturb anybody, far too polite to speak the truth, who with the utmost skill avoids touching on the petty vices which he knows to flourish in his parish. His sermons are model sermons—he gives his people nothing to think about and nothing to do. I can see them listening with placid faces and dead hearts to his mellifluous accents, his flowing periods, his soft and bland tones—as he makes the road to heaven easy and comfortable to all about him. I cannot do that.

'What an awakening shall it be when both

pastor and people stand before the Judge and mutually accuse one another !—Let me make a request of you. Will you have the goodness at that day to hold me free from your blood, seeing I have not shunned to declare unto you the whole counsel of God ? Do not point your finger at me, and say I did not warn you.

'Once again I utter the last voice of Advent, "The Lord is at hand !" Let us go forth to meet Him.'

A strange silence fell upon the listening congregation. The solemn words of the preacher, coming straight from his overwrought heart—the passionate pleading of his strong, yet tremulous voice—the uplifted arm—the flashing eye—the pale, weary face, acted like a spell upon his hearers. When he had finished, a sigh of relief involuntarily escaped from their lips and echoed through the church. When at length they rose to go, there was an utter absence of the bustle and noise which usually marked the close of the morning's services.

It had been a great effort to the preacher, and yet a relief. It was painful to him to speak thus to people whom he really loved, and yet he could not otherwise satisfy his conscience and sense of duty.

He thought he must now, as soon as Hatter after his return could make the necessary arrangements, leave the place. The people would not care to listen to him any more; they would be mortally offended at his plain, homely way of speaking—would, perhaps, misinterpret his motives, and for ever shut their hearts against him. He must seek a more congenial sphere of action.

But he was utterly mistaken in his conjecture as to the effect of his sermon upon the people. On the following Monday he received a visit from Dr. Jolly, who had the chief practice in Pollington and its neighbourhood, and was beloved and respected equally by rich and poor. To catch a sight of his handsome, laughing face was as invigorating as a draught of champagne to a thirsty traveller. As soon as he entered a sick chamber the

invalid felt better, and began to inquire for
his clothes, that he might get up and go out.
The Plaintons had seen a good deal of him
and his family in various ways, as they were
to be found taking part in every good work.
Mrs. Jolly was an especial favourite of the
curate's.

When the doctor entered Plainton's room
on the day after the sermon, that habitual
look on his face, as if he had just finished a
laugh or were about to begin one, had given
place to an aspect a little more serious.

'I have come to thank you for your sermon
of yesterday. It is what we have wanted
for some time. But you must not be in
despair. You will find plenty of high-minded
people to back you up in your work, when
they know what they ought to do. Besides,
you must not injure your health,' he added,
taking a professional survey of Plainton's
face.

The curate's heavy eyes brightened, and he
smiled gratefully.

'You know our parish,' continued the

doctor, ' has been a widowed parish for some
years. The Hatters don't visit, on principle
—the Vicar because he likes smelling the
Zulus, and his wife because she wants more
time in which to spoil her child. But there,'
checking himself as he saw the pained
look on the curate's face, ' I know you do
not suffer any one to speak ill of the
Vicar.' Then, bursting into one of his
contagious laughs, he exclaimed : 'There's
a deal of human nature in man, as the
old woman said to her husband when he
affectionately broke her head with a quart-
pot. Ta-ta.' Leaving Plainton to seek out
the meaning of his abstruse parable, he disappeared.

No one took offence at the much-talked-of
sermon, and during the following week more
cards were left at Plainton's lodgings, and he
received more invitations, than during the
previous three months. Every one greeted
him with genuine cordiality, and to his intense
surprise he found that, so far from exciting
opposition or wrath, his sermon had won the

hearts of many who before seemed utterly indifferent to religious influences. People whom he scarcely knew went out of their way to show they appreciated what he said, and to assure him they would help him in whatever way they could.

The disheartened curate was touched by all this unaffected and heartfelt kindness, and his hopes of being of use in Pollington were greatly raised. Instead of putting his letter of resignation into the post, he threw it into the fire.

CHAPTER X.

A NIGHT ADVENTURE.

ONE Sunday in the latter part of the winter, Plainton preached a sermon against gambling. He had become acquainted with the fact that betting and gaming were indulged in privately to a considerable extent. Towards the close of his discourse he observed the verger go from the vestry to the porch with a glass of water, and at the end of the service he inquired who had been unwell.

'The young lady, sir, who comes occasionally from Dargal Lodge. She said she had not been very well lately, and the heat of the church from the hot-water-pipes overpowered her.'

Plainton had not seen Miss Melody for the last few weeks—only once since the evening spent at Dargal Lodge already referred to. On hearing of this indisposition he called a day or two after. She was not to be seen, but Mrs. Melody presently came in with swollen eyes, and began sobbing as soon as she saw the curate.

'Oh! Mr. Plainton, Mona is so ill.'

'Why, what is the matter?'

'It is all owing to her being out so late on the water. Night after night all through the autumn she and her brother would stay out till it was quite dark, and then come in shivering. She suffers intensely just now.'

'A touch of rheumatism, I suppose.'

'Partly that, I think. But she has such dreadful pains in her side, and at times quite gasps for breath. Yet even now, if she is not watched, she will open her window at night and stare at the stars as if she were spellbound. I went to her room last night and found the maid asleep, but there was Mona out of bed standing by the open window ; and when I asked why she would be so foolish, she merely replied :

'"I was only listening to the stars, mamma dear."

'"Listening to the stars! child, what can you hear ?"

'"Many things about you and somebody else," she said, and then I could not get another word out of her.'

When Plainton took his departure he left a kindly message for the invalid, and in answer to Mrs. Melody's earnest entreaty promised to call again soon.

He did so in the following week. Miss Melody was better, but still keeping her bed. Her mother asked him to go upstairs and read to her. Plainton was pleased to find that she was not looking so ill as he expected. Her face was a little more pallid than usual, and she was evidently very weak, but otherwise there was no apparent difference.

After this Margaret called, and found her fast recovering. A little later they met her driving with her brother through Brackley

Park. A few days afterwards they received
an invitation to dinner, brought by Arthur in
person.   Margaret was engaged to Mrs.
Bridge, and could not go.   Plainton was unwilling to go without his sister, but Arthur
pleaded so earnestly that he consented.

The social festivity was in honour of Mona's
recovery, who quite seemed to have regained
her strength, and was in excellent spirits.
The curate left about ten o'clock, and took his
usual way home by the river.   It was a
bright night, but dark clouds were moving
swiftly across the sky.   There was a broad
path close to the stream, separated from the
adjoining property by a deep ditch.   He
walked on, admiring intensely the grotesque
shadows made by the trees, and the silvery
ripples of the water beneath the moon's
rays.

Suddenly he was confronted by a woman,
who said in an agitated voice :

'Oh ! Mr. Plainton, excuse me, sir, but
my husband is dying, and cries out day and
night for you ; will you come to him ?'

'Certainly,' said he, recovering from the surprise the unexpected apparition of the woman had caused him; 'but where is he?'

'It is some distance from here,' said the woman evasively; 'but I have a boat, if you don't mind.'

'A boat! then you do not live in Pollington. Why not go to your own clergyman? I have no right to visit the sick in another man's parish.'

'We cannot send for him, and my husband will have no one else but you. He knows you. He was in the same house in Bott's Lane last summer when you visited a man in consumption, and he raves about you now he is ill and cannot live;' and the woman sobbed bitterly.

'Well,' said Plainton, rather suspecting her story, 'give me your address, and I will call to-morrow.'

'Oh! no; that will be too late, sir. Do come now; it will be quite safe.'

'I am not afraid, my good woman, of going

anywhere at any time if I can be of use, but I must know where it is.'

' I cannot give you the address, sir, and you would not find it by yourself if I did.' Then, speaking in a low tone, she added, ' He's in trouble with the police, and will be taken from me if it is known where he is.'

_ These last words explained the mystery attending the woman's proceedings, and Plainton no longer hesitated.

' Very well, I will come.'

' Thank you, sir,' said she, gratefully, and they walked on.

' But how did you know,' said he, suddenly stopping again, ' where to find me ?'

' A friend at—in Pollington,' she replied, hesitating, ' told me you were expected at the Lodge to-night ; and my brother, who is with the boat, has often seen you go this way home. So I came and waited near the Lodge, and followed you.'

The curate wondered who the friend was, but said nothing. A few yards farther on they found the boat under the bank, and two men sitting near it smoking short pipes. Plainton kept his eye on the movements of the men, and did not attempt to get in until one was actually seated. He then assisted the woman on board and followed her. The first man, who he conjectured from what passed was the brother, took the bow oar, while the second, who answered to the name of Skittles, held the other. The woman manipulated the rudder-strings, and seemed thoroughly to understand their use.

The men were muffled up a good deal about the neck, and carefully avoided all Plainton's efforts to see their faces. Very little was spoken on the journey, except by the woman in giving some few necessary directions to the rowers. The moon was now no longer visible, and they had to proceed at times with great caution.

Plainton knew the river for some distance in daylight, but after passing the lock above Tonford, where they found the keeper apparently waiting for them, the ground was almost new to him, and the darkness baffled him. He recognised, however, one or two landmarks, such as the thick-set trees on the right, the two small islands in the centre of the stream, and the flat, open country on the left. But beyond these all was strange to him.

After a long pull they turned up a narrow stream, passed under some bare trees, and brought the boat to at a landing-place, where it was made fast. Plainton got out first and helped the woman, the men remained behind. She led the way along a narrow path for some distance, which brought them into a road, where they came upon a row of small houses. At the end of these was a narrow lane, which led to a field in the midst of which stood two cottages. The curate's guide tapped at the window of the first, and after some little delay, a young girl opened the door. The woman hastily mounted some stairs, and Plainton followed. In a small, wretchedly-furnished bedroom he found a man lying upon a couch, with his head and left arm bound up. He looked eagerly at the curate as he entered, and became much excited.

' Now, Jem dear, here's Mr. Plainton come on purpose to see you.'

' I knew he'd come. Give me some drink, Peg, and I'll speak to him.'

'Don't talk much, Jem ; let the gentleman talk instead,' said she coaxingly, as she gave him some lemonade out of a broken jug.

' I must—I must speak !' he exclaimed, vainly endeavouring to raise himself. ' I have hell-fire burning inside me !'

The curate took his hand and tried to calm him. After a while he knelt down and prayed earnestly. The man joined in the Lord's Prayer in a low tone. When Plainton rose from his knees, the sick man asked him to sit close by, as he had something to say.

' You needn't tell the gentleman anything, Jem,' said the woman, leaning over him.

' Be quiet, Peg. I am dying. I must speak.'

Then, in broken tones, and with many pauses through weakness, he told his course of crime. The curate was astonished to hear

that this man had been one of the accomplices
concerned in the great robbery of the Mort-
ley jewels, which made such a stir at the time
it happened, and that three daring burglaries
lately committed in the neighbourhood had
been planned and carried out by him. He
by no means looked as if he had ever been
equal to such a task. So far as Plainton
could judge, he was somewhat below the
middle height, and his face lacked the low,
brutal characteristics of feature usually as-
sociated with criminals of the lowest class.

It appeared from his confession that he had
taken a room, in the summer, in Bott's Lane,
in order to gather information about the residents. He had even been admitted a member
of a club combining conviviality with philan-
thropy, which was held at the Davenport Arms,
where he had met several of the servants of
the best houses in Pollington ; and from these,
over a friendly glass of grog, he had obtained
many valuable items of intelligence as to the
habits of various families, the disposition of
their rooms, and the very careful precau-

tions they took to frustrate the efforts of burglars. He had actually supped with the too-confiding servants in the very houses he had afterwards robbed. It was while living in Bott's Lane that he had seen the curate coming to the house, and heard him talk to an invalid in the next room of God, of Christ, and the Life Everlasting.

After his long recital of crimes, the man was evidently relieved, though exhausted by the effort, and Plainton used all his powers to direct his thoughts to the only Rock of Safety amidst the boiling waves of a restless conscience and the troubled memories of oft-repeated sin. He further showed him that if he were really repentant he must make what restitution he could, and asked if the property he had taken were all disposed of. The man replied that it was not, but that it was entirely out of his reach now.

Conversation at last became difficult, as his mind began to wander; and as he seemed disposed to sleep, Plainton prepared to depart.

When he went downstairs he said to the woman :

'Tell me how to get into the highway, and I will walk back. I will not trouble the men with the boat at this time of night.'

'You cannot do it, sir. It's too far round, and you'd never find it. The men must go back to Pollington to-night—one lives there, and the other farther down.'

'But how about getting through the lock ?'

'That's all right, sir. You will find the keeper waiting for you.'

Plainton then remembered for the first time that Margaret would be alarmed at his long absence, and he became anxious to return as quickly as possible.

The two men were ready with the boat, and, although they spoke but little, he could see they were anxious to be civil to him. The man whom Plainton conjectured to be Skittles took a pair of sculls, and the other went to the rudder. They passed through the lock without a word being exchanged on either side.

They then shot rapidly down the stream, Plainton acting as look-out. He was landed near the spot at which he had embarked. As he left the boat he managed to catch a near sight of the face of the man with the sculls, and he felt sure he had seen it before. He did not get to his lodgings until after one in the morning; and found his sister almost beside herself with terror, fearing some accident had happened.

'Oh! what has been the matter? And how pale you are!'

'There is nothing the matter with me, Margaret,' replied he quietly; 'I was called away to a dying man.'

She said no more. She knew her brother had had some strange experiences in his previous curacy as well as at Pollington, and she was always careful never to intrude into the secrets belonging to his work as a spiritual physician.

Some time after this adventure the curate

and his sister were dining at Dargal Lodge to commemorate Arthur's birthday. Mrs. Eugénie Constantine was there, with some musical friends from town, and sat on Plainton's right. A man to assist the servants and wait at table had been engaged for the evening.

' Hock or claret, sir ?' said he in the curate's ear.

' Hock, please.'

The man's hand trembled so much that Plainton thought it advisable to hold his wine-glass firmly at the bottom, whilst it was being filled. But as the waiter was raising the bottle again, it suddenly fell on an adjoining champagne glass, and shivered it to pieces.

' Be careful, Parker !' exclaimed Mrs. Eugénie. ' I hope you are not damaged, Mr. Plainton ?'

' Not in the least, thank you.'

Plainton tried to cover up the accident with a little pleasantry. But he was curious to know what was the matter with the man

—perhaps he was unwell, or had been sitting up all night with a sick wife or child. When he came to the opposite side of the table, the curate took a good look at him, and in spite of dress suit, elaborate shirt-front and white tie, recognised the features of Skittles, the companion of his midnight expedition.

CHAPTER XI.

AT THE BOAT RACE.

In a small cottage adjoining the Green, known as Shakespeare Villa, resided Miss Desdemona Corbyn, already mentioned. She was a lady of uncertain age, but with very marked characteristics, and came to live at Pollington—or rather condescended to exist there—with her friend Miss Snufton, who was some few years her senior.

Miss Corbyn's father had held a lucrative and high position under Government, had lived up to his income, and at his death left to his wife and daughter a miserable pittance to live on. At the death of her mother, Miss Corbyn took pity on Miss Snufton's loneli-

ness and joined in housekeeping with her.
Miss Snufton gratefully received her.

Miss Corbyn was peculiar in her appearance and manners. The female form is
generally regarded as affording some of the
more beautiful studies of Nature's curves and
graceful lines. Miss Corbyn was superior to
curves. When she stood upright, which she
generally did, except when chastising one of
her little dogs, she exhibited an almost perfect instance of a mathematical line. When
she graciously received a stranger, which she
seldom did unless the individual was considered a distinguished personage, it could not
be said that she *bowed*, for the very term
implies a figure of which Miss Corbyn was
incapable. It might be said with more truth
that she *angled*, that is to say, the upper part
of the mathematical line inclined towards the
lower and an obtuse angle was the result.

Miss Corbyn conceived that she was a very
great lady, though too often an unappreciated
one. She thought herself an infallible authority on manners, deportment, high breeding

and education, and was a fluent exponent of
'Debrett's Peerage.' The first time Plainton
called on her, she gave him a minute account
of the various high ecclesiastical personages
she had met at dinner, and produced an
assortment of old envelopes addressed to her
in years past by various eminent persons or
their relatives.

A little incident which happened when she
first gave Pollington the privilege of seeing
her, will help the reader to understand her
perfect appreciation of high breeding. Mrs.
Langley, who knew the Corbyns in earlier
days, had pressed the Broughams to call on
her. The Broughams had no desire to extend
the number of their acquaintances, but to
please good Mrs. Langley at last consented to
do so.   Miss Corbyn, being a new-comer, had
never heard of the Broughams, nor of their
connections ; and when they called, the mathematical line received them without an angle.
It remained perfectly upright, and at length
gave utterance to these words :

'I do not know by what right you presume

to call on me. I do not know you, and
have already a sufficient number of acquaintances.'

The Broughams, as soon as they had in a
degree recovered their breath after this cour-
teous and ladylike reception, explained that
at the desire of Mrs. Langley they had called,
otherwise they would not have done so. Soon
afterwards they took their leave.

In justice to Miss Corbyn, it remains to
be added that when she discovered the position of the Broughams in Pollington, and
was told of the high appointments held by
members of the family, she made three suc-
cessive calls on her visitors, and at last gain-
ing admittance, explained in gracious and
superabundant language that her reception of
them was under a misapprehension.

Miss Corbyn kept six small dogs, which
gave her a great deal of trouble. For she
was very intent upon teaching them to lead a
highly moral, if not ascetic life. They would
dutifully obey her injunctions for a considerable time, but just when she thought they

were beginning to see the advantages of high
breeding, they would, as if by a previous
arrangement, all fall into vicious courses and
exhibit the most plebeian inclinations. Early
every morning Miss Corbyn took out her
canine pupils, and Plainton often saw her
trying to persuade them to march in an
orderly and high-bred manner in front of her,
and heard her instructing them in the duties
of their high station.   But as all dogs have a
great deal of the canine nature in them, Miss
Corbyn's were not wholly above the influences
which attract others of their species, and a
stray bone, a chance lamp-post, or the gate or
corner of a house, would often prove too
much for their principles, and Miss Corbyn's
strict and highly moral maxims were then
wholly disregarded.

Her dogs were all named after the planets
or the gods and goddesses of classic mythology,
and Miss Corbyn's commands sounded very
odd to the curate's ears till he got quite used
to hearing them.

'Georgium Sidus!' she would exclaim in

the tone of an irate drill-sergeant, ' keep your
tail up, sir ! Venus I how dare you ! Leave
that dirty bone instantly ! Oh, Pallas
Athenæ I you abominable creature ! You
shall have dry bread and water for a week !'

Sometimes one or two of these highly-
cultured curs would be so ungrateful and
rebellious as to run away for a whole day and
night, and one morning Plainton, with pro-
found astonishment, met Miss Corbyn run-
ning down the principal street of the village
without bonnet or hat, flourishing her parasol
in her hand, and calling out in agonised tones
at the corner of every lane :

' Georgium Sidus, darling ! Oh I where
are you ?'

Another peculiarity about Miss Corbyn,
which sometimes led to curious results, was
her absent-mindedness. She would sometimes begin a story and leave off abruptly in
the middle, having apparently forgotten
where she was. This forgetfulness often
exhibited itself in her dress. Frequently
in winter, when there was a hard frost, she

might be seen walking through the streets in white satin shoes, with a light straw hat on the back of her head tied under her chin with long blue ribands, and carrying in her hand her famous yellow silk parasol.

She was in the habit of carrying two pairs of gloves in her pocket, in addition to the pair she was wearing. These she continually changed, according to the position of the person she was visiting. The worst pair, which was of black kid and very dilapidated, she called 'Scrub,' and wore in railway carriages or when taking out her dogs. The second pair, lavender-coloured and somewhat the worse for wear, received the appellation of 'Tiddleum,' and was used in visiting her ordinary acquaintances. The third pair, of a delicate cream-colour, was known as 'High Tiddleum,' and reserved for calls upon the high personages who rejoiced in Miss Corbyn's friendship or condescended to receive her. Owing to the absence of mind with which she was afflicted, the gloves often got intermixed, and Miss Corbyn has been seen making a call on Lady Killiecrankie at Tonford with a black and ragged 'Scrub' on one hand and an exquisitely-fitting, cream-coloured 'High Tiddleum' on the other.

The day before the Oxford and Cambridge Boat Race, Miss Plainton was rather surprised to receive a visit from Miss Corbyn, for their intercourse had been hitherto of the most formal character. Her visitor made a long, rambling, incoherent statement, getting into several fogs in the course of it, from which Margaret at length gathered that Miss Corbyn was strongly of opinion that Plainton and his sister were her cousins, through the Pawleys of Long Hazeldean, whom she had heard her late darling mother say were her own uncle's near relatives. Miss Corbyn, upon this discovery, which Margaret was in no position to dispute, made many bewildering calculations, which Margaret was wholly unable to follow. At the end of her apparently purposeless interview, she observed, as she rose to go, that Miss Snufton and herself, with three other young ladies, were going to the boat race the next morning, and if Mr. Plainton liked to join them, Miss Snufton would be glad to see him to breakfast at half-past seven o'clock.

Margaret gave the message to her brother when he came in, and remarked that she had heard in the morning that Miss Corbyn had already made the like kind offer to Fred Monmouth, Harry Templeton, and young Mr. Langley, but they had each declined.

Plainton said that five young ladies ought not to go to the boat race alone, and he thought he ought to go, especially, he added, laughing, as Miss Corbyn had claimed relationship with them.

'Well, you need not make any insinuations as to their age, Pawley ; and unless you wish to go, I do not think they are likely to be molested.'

'I don't know,' said he doubtfully ; 'you cannot be sure as to what might happen without an escort. There is no telling what Miss Corbyn's high spirits might lead her to do. Harry Templeton says she is a giddy young thing, and wants looking after ; but perhaps he was joking. I had better go.'

Plainton accordingly sent word over that he should be happy to come to breakfast in the morning. He arrived at the villa a few minutes before the hour named, but found that in their excitement his fair entertainers had finished breakfast some time. 'But,' said Miss Corbyn, 'you are just in time for a biscuit and some milk, which I was about to give to Georgium Sidus, who, however, has been naughty.'

Plainton helped the ladies into the open fly which presently arrived, and then mounted the box with the driver.

They arrived at the railway bridge without any incident calling for remark, unless it was the regularity with which Miss Corbyn stopped the carriage to make odd and incoherent inquiries of any passing policeman.

The ladies of the expedition all wore Oxford colours, as Miss Corbyn's nephew was rowing in that boat. As soon as the carriage

had taken up its position, Miss Corbyn became greatly excited. She had been favoured
with tickets to admit her on to the bridge,
and as soon as it was announced that the
boats had started, she was seized with an
irresistible desire to try a position there. At
her request the curate scrambled with her up
the bank, and mounted the railway bridge.
This lofty coign of vantage delighted her.
She stood looking into the water for some
time, trying to catch the first glimpse of the
Oxford crew, and not seeing them, began
to clamber on to the parapet. Plainton
earnestly advised her not to be so rash, as
if the crowd became much thicker she
might be pushed over. Miss Corbyn apparently did not hear, but continued her
climbing. Her escort was at his wits' end.
What could he do? He could not venture
on the liberty of pulling her back—he had
not spoken to her more than twice before.
He could only argue and entreat. But his
eloquence was all thrown away. Miss Corbyn
made many remarks on the likelihood of her

nephew's boat winning, but her observations were apparently addressed to the river, and Plainton remained unnoticed and unanswered, though he did not cease to ply his expostulations.

Presently, Miss Corbyn, finding her position uncomfortable, gradually drew her feet up on to the stone-work. The perspiration stood out on the curate's forehead, and shouting out:

'Good gracious! Miss Corbyn, are you going to commit suicide?'—took hold of her by the waist and tried to pull her back.

In vain. Miss Corbyn had by this time got her face to the stream, looking towards the starting-place, and her feet were dangling over the water.

Notwithstanding Plainton's mental agony, he heard the stoker of the engine which had pulled up on the bridge remark to the driver: 'I say, Jim, the parson's gal *is* a plucky un.'

'My eye!' returned the driver; 'she'll have him over before he has her back.'

Her excitement was intense. The Cambridge boat had now turned the corner, and

the Oxford boat had not appeared. Whereupon Miss Corbyn uttered a heart-rending
wail of anguish, and exclaimed :

'Oh! my nephew! my nephew! he is
drowned and lost! What shall I do? The
boat is upset, and gone to the bottom!' and
clasping her hands, she gazed upwards in
despair.

But just then the Oxford boat appeared.
An instantaneous change was wrought in
Miss Corbyn. She screamed with delight,
clapped her hands, and kicked her heels
against the stone-work.

Her unhappy companion, fearing that she
would clap herself over, frantically held on to
her immovable waist with both hands, shouting into the small of her back with all his
might :

'You mad-woman! Come back! come
back!'

But he might as well have addressed the
nymphs of the Thames—or the Fates—or the
Furies. Miss Corbyn heard nought but her
own shrill scream.

She had been clapping her hands, still holding her parasol in one of them ; but discovering that it interfered with her energy, she hastily put it under her arm. In so doing, she accidentally knocked off Plainton's hat, which luckily fell between him and the bridge, and putting his foot on the crown he prevented it travelling any further.

But the parasol still interfered with Miss Corbyn's demonstrations. Suddenly she turned her head, and said :

' Hold my parasol, please, Mr. Plainton.'

But his hands were both engaged, which she apparently did not perceive. Looking down, however, upon his open mouth, as he shouted in his agony and terror, she saw a vacant and convenient space, and accordingly lodged the sunshade between his teeth, effectually putting an end to his ineffectual entreaties.

When the boats had passed under the bridge, Miss Corbyn grew calm, and coolly took up her parasol again as if from its accustomed receptacle. Then with great dexterity throwing her feet up on to the bridge, was dragged on to the platform by her exhausted companion.

He perceived that she had lost one of her boots, but said nothing. He was completely done up with the fruitless struggle and mental pain she had caused him. Picking up his smashed hat, he tried to press it into shape. Miss Corbyn, putting her hands to her sides, and taking a long breath, remarked :

'You need not have held me quite so tight, Mr. Plainton.'

But the curate did not hear her. He was thinking of the moment when he should again be free, and making resolutions as to his attendance at future boat-races with his present company.

'I never will again,' he said aloud, quite unconsciously, 'as long as I live. No, never !'

'Thank you !' she replied quite graciously ; 'it was quite an accident, I am sure.'

They began to walk along the platform, when Miss Corbyn discovered that one of her boots was missing.

'Oh! I am robbed ! Thieves ! Pickpockets !

Police !' she shouted, dexterously holding up her bootless foot, and clasping her hands at the same moment. 'Some one has stolen my boot !'

A few of the bystanders who had enjoyed her demonstrations on the bridge began to gather round.

Plainton took hold of her arm, and dragging her along, exclaimed angrily :

'You Bedlamite ! You dropped it into the water !'

'Did I ?' she asked in a tone of innocent and childlike surprise ; 'dear me ! how strange ! how remarkable !' Waving her arm and placing herself in a theatrical attitude, she said, 'Let us go and see if it has floated to the bank, or if some lucky boatman has picked it up.'

But Plainton, wiping his forehead, was still repeating his newly-formed resolution—

'Never again ! never ! never !'

'Perhaps it would be useless,' cheerfully rejoined his companion.

They came to the carriage, Miss Corbyn

leaning on the curate's arm whilst she hopped on one foot and held the other bootless one at a considerable elevation in front of her. He opened the door, put her in, and shut it.

'Oh! Mr. Plainton,' said Miss Snufton, 'you are to come inside going back. We can make room for you.'

But Plainton, pale and tired, was looking across the carriage into the river—

'No! never again, as long as I live!' he vacantly repeated.

Miss Snufton caught a part of his words, and noticed the strange look in his face. Turning to Miss Corbyn, she observed that Mr. Plainton seemed quite lost, and would be the better for a glass of wine. Thereupon that heroic and energetic lady, rattling the handle of her parasol on the crown of the curate's hat, placed her other hand to her mouth, and shouted at the top of her voice, ending in a sort of prolonged sea-gull scream:

'Hi! hi! hi! Mr. Plain—ton! Get inside, and have a glass of wi—ne!'

But that unhappy man was quite uncon-

scious of the tattoo of the parasol and of the
screech of his fair companion's cracked voice :
he was still absently thinking of future boat-
races.

'No ! never again, as long as I live,
never !' he murmured, and lifting his hat to
the ladies, slowly disappeared amongst the
crowd.

'Dear me ! what a strange man, Desdemona !'

'Yes, it's excitement.   He was a thousand
times worse on the bridge, and would have
pushed me over if I had not clung to the
parapet.   He was quite mad for the time.'

'Oh ! my dear ! what a merciful escape
you have had !'

'Yes, indeed !'

Towards the middle of the following week,
when Plainton came in from a long parish
round, Margaret said :

'Mrs. Sowerby has been here with three
of her daughters to offer you her congratulations.'

'Indeed !' said he wearily, 'I am much

obliged to her, but I shall be better pleased when I know what it is for.'

'I am not so sure about that. Mrs. Sowerby congratulates you upon your engagement, and would like to know if the day is fixed, and who are to be the bridesmaids?'

'What does the woman mean?' he asked in a tone of horror, and with a look of terror.

'No! it is what do *you* mean? They say that no two men ever made love in the same manner, and you certainly are pre-eminently original—to choose a railway bridge, with a crowd upon it, and then, in the delighted gaze of applauding thousands, to put both your arms round the waist of a young, confiding girl, and to lean your head over her shoulder and kiss her repeatedly; what could it mean from a man of your years and in your position, if it did not mean matrimony?'

Plainton covered his face with his hands and groaned. His misery was past speech. The whole scene on the bridge came up before his mental vision, and for the first time it occurred to him to imagine what its effects might be on a spectator at a little distance. He groaned again, and muttered through his fingers :

'How dreadful!'

'Ah!' said his sister, 'you should have thought of the consequences before. You cannot go back now. . Besides, half the parish witnessed it. Charming Desdemona! Ah!' continued Margaret, looking out of the window, 'here comes Mrs. Chubb and her daughter, no doubt to offer *her* congratulations. Yes, and I see across the green Miss Piggott, followed by Mrs. Chine in the dim distance. We shall have a house full!'

Plainton retreated to his bedroom, still groaning.

CHAPTER XII.

A TESTIMONIAL, AND WHAT CAME OF IT.

PLAINTON regularly sent Mr. Hatter the parish news, and continued to receive instructions on the most minute portions of his work. Many of these could not possibly be carried out, but as far as was practicable the curate loyally observed the Vicar's wishes, even when they were wholly contrary to his own experienced judgment.

After staying a few weeks on the Continent, Mr. Hatter had proceeded to the Holy Land, not to visit the holy places, for they had no attractions for him, but to collect items for a new work he was preparing for the press, and which he thought would suffi-

ciently hit the public taste for the marvellous
or unknown to sell well and more than reim-
burse him for his outlay in travelling and
sight-seeing.

His ardour in pursuing this laudable object had led him to explore the country on
the east of the Jordan and the Dead Sea, a
district so often referred to by writers as unknown or little visited. It was here he
elaborated the plan of his new work. He
passed through Moab with some little difficulty, then turning northwards traversed the
plain of Haouran and the wild region of the
Szaffa, as far as was practicable. Turning back
towards the Jordan he had come upon the
Zurka, the course of which he followed towards its most southerly source.

Plainton had not heard from him for some
time, when he received a long letter stating
that the Vicar had taken up his abode at
Amman, the site of the ancient Rabbah, where
he had made some most important discoveries,
which he confidently affirmed would necessi-
tate the re-writing of a large portion of

ancient history, and would completely revolutionise our views of the early civilisation of the world.

In digging amongst the ruins of Rabbah, he had discovered the remains of a city far more ancient than that celebrated capital of the Ammonites, and had come upon vestiges of a civilisation extending back to an era far beyond even that of the Zamzummims, who had held the country previous to its occupation by the Ammonites. He was now making arrangements to bring away copies of the tablets and inscriptions upon which he had so happily lighted. As soon as this work was completed he should return to England, in order to give to the world without delay the results of his successful labours. He expected to be in Pollington by the beginning of April, if not before.

In the meanwhile, Plainton had been steadily pursuing his pastoral work with more of quietude and satisfaction than he had yet experienced. Unknown to himself or sister, the principal members of the congregation determined to give the curate some tangible proof of their regard. The church wardens took the matter in hand with such zeal, that in a few days the sum of ninety pounds was subscribed to be presented by the churchwardens as a slight mark of respect and esteem from the members of the congregation.

The whole business was managed quietly, and without the least ostentation. One morning, Mr. Thornycroft and Mr. Manley, the two churchwardens, called at the curate's lodgings, and handing the purse over to him, the former gentleman said :

'We bring this as a mark of the regard the congregation have for you, and in appreciation of your indefatigable labours during the absence of the Vicar. We could easily have collected double the amount, but as Mr. Hatter returns next week, we thought we would settle the matter so as not to trouble him.'

'And we wish you to understand,' added Mr. Manley, speaking slowly and emphatically, 'that this sum is presented irrespective

and independent of your stipend as curate of
Pollington. Two offertories are given every
year towards the Curate's Fund, but this is a
testimonial intended to be altogether distinct
from that.'

Although the money itself was most acceptable—for the curate and his sister had
been compelled latterly to abstain from firing
and meat in order to make their scanty means
sufficient—Plainton was most grateful for the
strong proof this testimonial afforded of the
respect in which he was held. If these
people so regarded him, he argued, would he
not be able in time to influence them in
spiritual matters, and lead them on to that
highest life to realise which had been the
aspiration alike of his childhood, youth, and
manhood ?

Mr. Hatter returned a fortnight before
Easter. The church was prettily decorated
at that Queen of festivals, but Plainton
sorely regretted the cost to the church furniture, and to the tempers of those concerned.

The pulpit had been the victim of new and

various designs ever since it had been erected, and there was scarcely a square inch of the wood not disfigured with the marks of nails. Portions of the carving had been completely split away. The stone-work within the chancel had also suffered considerably, and large portions had been chipped away before the nails could be driven in sufficiently securely to hold the wreaths.

The curate had not had a moment's peace since the decorations had been taken in hand. First of all the money to defray the expenses had to be collected, then some division made of the flowers amongst the workers. Jealousy and dissatisfaction were the chief result. Margaret complained that Miss Corbyn had appropriated the best flowers, that Miss Piggott had run off with some of the finest wire, and that the Sowerbys were in high dudgeon because they had not been asked to decorate the chancel, but only to make the wreaths for the nave.

Plainton's life was a burden to him the whole week through with these complaints and petty squabbles, and he remarked to Miss Langley, who was the very personification of meekness and amiability, that people in this world were not highly christianised enough to undertake decorations, but possibly they might become equal to it after a cycle of ages spent in another and better sphere.

The Vicar was in a perpetual fume the whole time the work was going on. He would come into the church while the workers were busy, and have continual altercations all round. The meek and quiet ones fared worst. He bullied and insulted them till they left the church. The Broughams, however, parried his cynical remarks with interest. Once Plainton came in and found him pale and trembling with rage, because they flatly refused to carry out his suggestions as being utterly incongruous and absurd. To relieve his heated feelings Hatter rushed to the vestry and tied a wet towel round his head. But usually he avoided quarrelling with the Broughams, or abjectly begged their pardon immediately afterwards, for he was anxious to keep on good terms with them, as their brother was an intimate friend of Lord Greyling's.

It was in the week following Easter week, that Mr. Hatter, in a soft, unctuous tone, invited Plainton to breakfast. The curate did not like these affectionate invitations to partake of his Vicar's hospitality. Breakfast had been hitherto invariably followed by a long interview in which the Vicar propounded something mean or dishonourable, or threw obstacles in the way of projected work. Plainton had no option but to accept the proffered hospitality, but he went to the Vicarage on the appointed morning with many misgivings. Mr. and Mrs. Hatter both received him with marked attention, and the curate felt sure some subtle mischief was a-foot.

'Hetty,' said the Vicar, as they were proceeding to breakfast, 'give Mr. Plainton this beautiful bunch of flowers.'

Hetty obeyed. The curate remembered that this very process had always preceded

something particularly disagreeable and offensive.

Mr. Hatter complimented him on his work
during the meal, and deferred continually to
his opinion, contrary to his usual custom,
which was to contradict any assertion, however obvious and true, the curate might venture to make.

Breakfast ended, Hatter invited Plainton
into his study, and gave him a chair. He
then said with tremulous voice and moist
eyes :

'I cannot tell you how much I value your
services, and what a comfort it has been to
have you here during my absence. Eh—eh
—I am glad also to see that—eh—eh—the
people also are beginning to appreciate you—
eh—so pleased to find they have given you a
present. I only wish it had been double the
amount—and that was one thing I wanted to
see you about. You—eh—remember that—
eh—eh—I undertook to give you one hundred pounds a year, and the congregation
were to give you the other thirty pounds ?'

'I understood that I was to receive one hundred and thirty pounds, and that part was raised by the congregation through an offertory once a year.'

'Exactly. There has always been a difficulty in getting them to do their part. I am sure I am very pleased to see that they are now beginning to understand their duty in this respect. Eh—eh—you have been here a year, and the thirty pounds I have already paid you beyond the one hundred pounds has come nearly all out of my own pocket—for the sermon did not realise a great deal—you can therefore now return it to me; or, if it is more convenient, you may consider that thirty pounds out of the quarter's salary just due to you has been paid—you can give me the receipt before you go—and that thirty pounds for the ensuing year has also been advanced by the congregation. I will make a note to that effect which we can both sign. There remains thirty pounds, which I do not intend to touch, although I might very fairly claim it, seeing that up to

11—2

the present time the congregation have done next to nothing to help me. I might justly consider that that remaining thirty pounds is a subscription paid two years in advance. However, I prefer to be generous rather than stand on my technical rights. You shall keep that balance, so that by this transaction you make a clear gain of thirty pounds. It is no more than you deserve. I am very glad indeed to feel that our people are rising up to their responsibilities. It is really very good of them to come to my aid so handsomely. I think with judicious management we may get them to fork over pretty liberally in the future.'

The Vicar paused. Plainton had not attempted to interrupt him as he elaborated his views as to the meaning of the testimonial. Hatter remained sitting at the table, carefully brushing into a little heap some crumbs of biscuit, as if he had already before him the gold pieces presented to the curate. At length the latter mildly objected :

'But that is not what the people meant.

They expressly said it was to be independent of my engagement with you, and of any sum already agreed on between us.'

'Eh—eh—' gasped Hatter, casting a malignant glance at Plainton, 'the law does not allow a congregation to come between a Vicar and his curate. Properly speaking, the whole sum belongs to me ; but after deducting the thirty pounds I have already paid you on their behalf, I am quite willing to consider the remaining sixty pounds as the amount raised by them for the ensuing year.'

Plainton felt that all this was very disgusting and unutterably mean. He watched the avaricious face of the man as he sat at the table. It was quite a study worthy of the brush of a Rembrandt. The whole features were lighted up with the passion of greed, the lines of the forehead contracted, the eyes glanced furtively at his victim, while the veins on his trembling hand seemed to swell up in anticipation of enjoying the lust of clutching that which was another's.

But Plainton had no heart to argue a

point of money with a brother clergyman, and that man his Vicar. He felt that between himself and the miserable fraction of a man before him an immeasurable gulf was fixed as regards notions of right and wrong, of honesty, honour, manliness, delicacy, good-feeling, and of every other quality which goes to the making up of the character of a gentleman.

He longed to get out of the tainted moral atmosphere of the Vicarage, and to breathe again the pure air of heaven.

He therefore simply said, 'Let it be as you say, provided you satisfy the church-wardens.'

'Oh! there is no difficulty about that.'

Plainton felt intensely relieved to get out-side.

When he told his sister what had happened she was overwhelmed with indignation and vexation.

'Oh! Pawley, after all these months' un-grudging labour on your part! After all your attention to his private affairs, his intricate money transactions and never-ending commissions ; after all your thankless toil at his book, your slavery from morning till night, to think that he should now come back and deliberately rob you of your little present from the people ! It is wrong of you to permit it. It is unfair to the congregation.'

'I feel it ought not to be. But I think it is more in accordance with the teaching of the Sermon on the Mount to suffer it than to resist and make a scandal in the church.'

'I am sure it cannot be right.'

'It is not right that he should take it, certainly ; but I must either let the wrong be done, or resign just when I am beginning to be of use.'

Plainton went out to walk by the river and consider what was his duty under these difficult circumstances. Whilst he was gone, Mrs. Jolly called, and Margaret told in her sympathetic ear what had occurred. Mrs. Jolly was greatly shocked.

'I knew he was an unscrupulous man,' she

said, 'but I never imagined he was equal to this.'

Before the day was over, the whole village was alive with the affair. The scandal Plainton had been so anxious to avoid had been precipitated by his desire to bear with the wrong.

CHAPTER XIII.

A LESSON IN LETTER-WRITING.

THE churchwardens had an interview with the Vicar, and argued the matter for some hours. But here Mr. Hatter had the advantage. Plainton had heard him say that any tactics are allowable in order to confute an adversary; and that any statement is justifiable if it helps to put him on a wrong scent. It must he confessed that Hatter consistently followed out this theory, and when known facts would not admit of being sufficiently manipulated to answer his purpose, he created other facts which would.

Hatter's skill of fence, his subtlety, his unscrupulousness, his habitual and daring untruthfulness, and his sophistic use of words, combined to aid him in puzzling two upright men who understood only plain English. He did not, however, get them to see that robbery, by whatever name it was called, was anything else than robbery. Hatter was evidently taken much aback by the stir which was likely to be made.

On the following Sunday night he again invited the curate to come to breakfast on Monday morning. Plainton hesitated. Hatter said :

' I am going away for a week, and I want to arrange some parish matters.'

The curate was obliged to accept the unwelcome invitation.

When he told Margaret, she exclaimed :

' Oh ! how I hate your going to that horrid house ! I never feel sure that you will come out alive. Don't let him talk you into anything contrary to your own common sense and better judgment. He is like the boa constrictor, and licks his victim all over before making a meal of him. Your last breakfast there cost you £60. You cannot afford many more at that price. It is some comfort to think that he can only rob you of what is left, unless he takes your clothes.'

The slimy process of the former week was repeated. The Vicar and his wife used the most oily flattery at breakfast, and Hetty brought him the usual propitiatory offering of flowers. Plainton wondered at this, for on Sunday the Vicar had been particularly rude to him, and had made a point of offering him a gross slight at the celebration of the Holy Communion. The curate had conjectured from these marks of ill-will that Mr. Hatter intended to have an angry interview, notwithstanding the invitation to breakfast.

If such had been the Vicar's intention it had given place to another more subtle plan.

He began by telling Plainton of the great excitement in the parish, and appealed to him to do all in his power to allay it. The latter replied that he deeply regretted that there should be any unpleasantness, especially over money matters, as it would tend to throw back his work in the parish.

'Exactly. I felt sure you would see it in that light. I know I need not appeal to your generosity to remove the false view the church-wardens take of the matter. I wish to act liberally in every way towards you. If I have done so at present only in words, it is because I have not yet had the opportunity of doing so in act. Lord Greyling—eh—eh—asked me the other day if I knew a fit man for a country living—eh—but I did not think it worth your acceptance. I am expecting to offer you something much better, if you decide not to succeed me here.'

'I am not anxious to have a living,' said Plainton, quietly.

'No, I know. But it might be your duty to accept—eh—eh—a higher sphere of work. Would you mind writing to the churchwardens to say you—eh—eh—regret this—eh—misunderstanding?'

'I think it would be better for me to see them. I can say much more by word of mouth than by letter.'

'Eh—eh—it would be better if you would write, as they could show the letter to the people. You cannot call on all yourself.'

'Well,' said Plainton, still hesitating, 'I will write, if you think it will make matters straight.'

'It is very good of you,' said Hatter, with trembling lips and tears in his eyes.

Plainton was distressed at his perturbation, and his generosity was excited by his apparently throwing himself into the curate's hands.

'Would you mind writing it now, as time presses, and I want to go to Brighton by the next train? Then the matter will be off my mind.'

The curate was rather surprised at this urgent request. Its indelicacy jarred upon him. He did not expect that he could do anything so gross, notwithstanding the many previous proofs he had received of the Vicar's utter disregard of the feelings and reputation of others, provided he could serve his own turn. The fact was, that Plainton was

always looking for gentlemanly feeling, high
honour, and nobleness of heart, in a man who
had never for a moment known in himself
what those qualities were. The Vicar noticed
his hesitation to comply with his request.

'Surely,' said he, 'you cannot object to
say what you have to say now, as well as at
any other time. Why should you object?'—
looking at him with one of his suspicious
glances.

'Well, if it will be any satisfaction to you,
and relieve your mind from its present burden—certainly I can say here what I have to
say as well as at home.'

'Thank you. Here's some paper. What
will you say?'

'I shall say that I regret ——'

'Eh—eh—I have drawn up here,' said
Hatter, pulling a sheet of paper out of his
pocket—'a few words which I think will
answer the purpose. Suppose you begin
thus :—

'"My dear Mr. Thornycroft,—Various
rumours have reached my ears respecting the

Vicar's conduct in the matter of the testimonial lately presented to me." '

'Yes,' said Plainton, 'that's quite true.'

'Perhaps you would not mind writing it before I go on.'

The curate did as he was requested. The Vicar continued :

' " I greatly regret the disturbance in the parish to which these injurious reports have given rise." '

'Certainly,' said Plainton, writing. 'I quite agree with that.'

The Vicar proceeded :

' " I therefore hasten to inform you that I quite acquiesce in the view which Mr. Hatter takes as to the disposal of the sum so kindly presented to me by the congregation, and I believe it to be an equitable arrangement." '

The curate put down his pen and looked thoughtfully at the paper, he then said :

'I do not think I can honestly write that. I told you the other day I would agree to your arrangement if you would undertake to satisfy the churchwardens. I gave no opinion as to its character.'

The Vicar bit his lip with vexation, and a gleam of bitter hate shot out of the corner of his eye. He restrained himself with a great effort, and said unctuously :

'I intend to satisfy the churchwardens. You acquiesced in my view last week, why do you not this ? Surely you do not want to head a popular outbreak against your Vicar ?'

'No ; but the words you have read do not honestly state my views.'

'Well, suppose you say :

'"I hasten to inform you that I quite acquiesce in the arrangement which Mr. Hatter has made with regard to the sum so kindly presented to me by the congregation." '

'Yes,' said the curate, doubtfully, 'I certainly have acquiesced in it.'

'You cannot then object to saying as much.'

Plainton wrote it down.

'Now, I do not know if you can be magnanimous enough to write the next sentence, but if you can I shall feel your kindness very deeply. It stands thus :

' " Mr. Hatter has hitherto treated me with kindness and consideration, and I have every reason to believe that he will act generously towards me in the future." '

' It is rather strong language, perhaps,' remarked the Vicar, ' but remembering the regard I have shown for your health, in sending you little presents of calomel pills when you have looked pale, and also the invitations I have given you to luncheon, together with the kind letters I have written to you from abroad—I think you might honestly say that I have treated you with kindness and consideration.'

' Yes, I can write that much,' said Plainton, who began to feel keenly the false position in which he had allowed himself to be placed.

' With regard to the future,' continued Hatter, ' I am making arrangements to provide a living for you. You are the best-fitted of any man I know to recommend to Lord Greyling, who is a connection of Mrs. Hatter's, and has several good livings in his gift. There are many things I hope to do for you in the future, and I trust you will be able to take my word for it. If you believe me, you cannot hesitate to say so. A man acts generously, you know, when he does more for another than he is obliged.'

Plainton was silent. How could he dispute Mr. Hatter's estimate of his own generosity?

Hatter watched every movement of the curate's face as a cat watches the useless efforts of a caged mouse.

'Do you doubt my word?' he asked, in his oiliest of tones.

'I am bound to believe your statement that you wish to act generously towards me.'

'Precisely. Then you cannot mind other people knowing the high opinion of me you are good enough to entertain.'

Plainton wrote the sentence. Hatter proceeded:

' " I shall feel obliged by your using your best efforts to pacify those members of the congregation who are dissatisfied with what has been arranged, and to contradict the reports to which I have referred.

'"Believe me,

'"Yours very sincerely,

'"Pawley Plainton."'

The curate wrote the above without further remark. Mr. Hatter eagerly fastened the letter in an envelope and gave it to Plainton to address. He then hastily seized it and put a stamp on it.

'Perhaps you will post it at once?'

'I will,' said Plainton, and departed. He felt he would have been stifled had he stayed longer in that vicious atmosphere. He was depressed and humiliated. As he passed the post-office he dropped in his letter with great misgivings, and then walked slowly to his lodgings, the mist clearing away from his mind at every step. He felt now that he had done a weak thing. He had allowed himself to be betrayed into writing a letter, which with the Vicar's glosses conveyed one meaning, but which without

them would present a very different aspect
to the minds of the readers for whom it was
intended.

Surely it had been enough that he had
acquiesced in the Vicar's act of spoliation ;
he ought not to be called upon by the spoiler
to defend the act as being in itself just, and
the arrangement made with regard to it as
being even generous. For although the
curate's letter did not thus characterise it,
he knew that the great majority of those
who read it would suppose that that was
what he meant.

CHAPTER XIV.

THE PUPIL IMPROVES HIS STYLE.

PLAINTON found Margaret anxiously awaiting his return. He briefly told her all that had happened. She was much moved.

'This is worse,' she said, 'than his robbing you of your money, for he is now taking away your character and destroying your keen discrimination between right and wrong. You may have been generous to him, but you are unfair to the people and untrue to yourself.'

'I certainly wish to be generous to him, but not at the expense of what is due to others. I have posted the letter, but I shall withdraw it. In fact, I will go at once to the Thornycrofts and tell them so. At the same time I hall request that nothing more be said about the matter. I shall also write to Hatter and tell him what I have done.'

Plainton found Mrs. Thornycroft at home, but not her husband. He told her that he had written a letter that morning to Mr. Thornycroft on the subject of the testimonial, which, on reflection, he desired to withdraw.

'It has not yet arrived,' said Mrs. Thornycroft, who saw that the curate was much disturbed ; 'but if you wait it will be here presently, and then you can have it.'

Mrs. Thornycroft was the daughter of a clergyman, and understood thoroughly the ins and outs of parish life. She had herself taken a district in Pollington, and had acted as superintendent of the Sunday-school until Mr. Hatter, in one of his fits of passion, publicly insulted her, when she resigned, which was probably what he wanted.

After the curate had waited about a quarter of an hour, the butler brought in a letter addressed to Mr. Thornycroft.

'That is your writing, I think,' said

Mrs. Thornycroft, handing Plainton the letter.

'Yes,' he replied, returning it.

'Oh! you may keep it. I will explain to Mr. Thornycroft.'

'You are very kind, but I think it is only right that you should read it before returning it to me, in case any question should arise as to its contents.'

'It is not necessary, but I will do so if you wish it.'

'Pray do.'

Mrs. Thornycroft read it slowly. When she had finished, she handed it to Plainton and remarked :

'I see it is written on a sheet of the Vicarage paper !'

'Yes, I wrote it at the Vicarage, at Mr. Hatter's request.'

'I see,' said Mrs. Thornycroft, looking compassionately at the curate. 'What would you like me to do ? If it will relieve your mind the fact of the letter need not be mentioned to another person.'

'I do not mind that, thank you. I must have it mentioned to Mr. Thornycroft, as it has been delivered at his house. But I wish that no action should be taken. Let it be considered that this letter has not been written.' He then tore it up, and put the pieces in the fire. 'Now, I earnestly beg that everybody concerned in the testimonial will let the matter rest. It will be impossible for me to stay in the place if there is to be any more bickering about the money.'

'Very well. I will tell Mr. Thornycroft.'

Plainton's mind was relieved. He had so far retraced his steps. He had intercepted his letter to the churchwardens and destroyed it. Only Mrs. Thornycroft had read it, and he could perfectly rely upon her discretion. To-morrow he would write to Hatter, and leave the letter at the Vicarage, so that he might have it as soon as he returned. During the day he saw Mr. Thornycroft and Mr. Manley, and gained from them a promise to do their best to pacify the parish.

He retired early to his room, but not to

sleep. He felt keenly the humiliation he had suffered in permitting himself to be dragged through the mire by his unscrupulous Vicar. Yet in suffering it, was he not fulfilling (he argued with himself) the precepts contained in the Sermon on the Mount ? Was he or was he not acting in accordance with the words :

' I say unto you, That ye resist not evil : but whosoever shall smite thee on thy right cheek, turn to him the other also. And if any man will sue thee at the law, and take away thy coat, let him have thy cloak also. And whosoever shall compel thee to go a mile, go with him twain.'

Plainton had no sleep that night. He tossed about from one side to the other till morning dawned, still discussing with his conscience the above nice points of casuistry. He rose unrested, but his mind was quite clear as to his duty.

He saw that if he executed all Hatter's injunctions there would not have been a shred of honour or honesty left him. He came also to the conclusion that the precepts of the

Sermon on the Mount could not be literally obeyed, under all circumstances, without perpetuating or sanctioning wrong-doing, which certainly could not be the intention of the great Lawgiver.

After breakfast he penned the following letter, and with a light heart left it at the Vicarage :

'Pollington Green,
'April 1, 18—.

'DEAR MR. HATTER,

'After leaving your house yesterday morning and reflecting upon the whole matter, I found myself unable to allow the churchwardens to have the letter which I had written at your house, and at your dictation. It was a very weak thing to do without consideration, and I blame myself for it exceedingly ; but my judgment was overborne by my feelings and your wishes. I have therefore destroyed the letter, and seen the churchwardens, as I first proposed, and I trust this painful matter will now drop.

'After a day and night's anxious thought, I have determined neither to say nor do anything more in the affair.

'My honour and independence must be preserved intact, come what may.

'Very faithfully yours,

'Pawley Plainton.'

The curate told the servant to give the letter to the Vicar as soon as he came back. His conscience was now clear. Hatter would no doubt rage like a wild beast, but that was of little consequence. Of the two, the curate would infinitely prefer the savagery of the wild beast to the slimy coils and subtle venom of the serpent.

The Vicar did not return till Saturday afternoon. On Sunday morning Plainton met him as he was going into the Sunday-school. The Vicar came up with an unctuous smile, holding out his hand in the most affectionate manner. He made no reference to the letter, but spoke of the Sunday-school work, attempted one or two feeble jokes, with a ghastly grimace, and accompanied his curate very officiously from one school to the other, paying him, as opportunity offered, various covert compliments.

Plainton was astonished. He expected they would have had a great encounter, which would have ended in his quietly withdrawing from the parish altogether—a consummation he would not regret now, as he felt more and more how impossible it was to work with Hatter and retain his integrity. He did not for a moment anticipate that the Vicar would swallow his letter whole without making a single wry face. It was evident, however, that whatever facial contortions he had executed in taking the bitter draught, he carefully intended to keep to himself.

A few days after this incident Margaret received a visit from Mrs. Grimm. Mrs. Horsman Grimm was the wife of a gentleman who held a lucrative position in the Encumbered Estates Court. She was in some respects original and peculiar. When she first came to Pollington she gave out that she intended to visit no one. The consequence was, as she shrewdly anticipated, that the exclusives of Pollington were all most anxious to make her acquaintance, and everybody called. She kept up a wholesome respect for her good opinion by alternately flattering and snubbing her friends. If they called upon her one day, she would receive them with genial courtesy; but if on the next she happened to meet them in the street, she would give them the cut direct. Besides this eccentricity, having a sharp tongue, she inspired a good deal of fear by ridiculing everybody to everybody else. The connections, mode of life, habits, appearance, speech, and individualities of every notable person in the place had received the honour of her full, free, and acrid criticism.

Mrs. Grimm further prided herself upon holding peculiar opinions on every known subject of interest. The following were some of her articles of faith: that she herself was lineally descended from Henry the Eighth; that the claimant to the Tichborne estates was the rightful heir; that typhoid fever was caused by the spots in the sun; that the Franco-German War was due to the aberrations of the Gulf Stream; that the depression in British trade might be traced to the scarcity of native oysters.

As the Plaintons had been very popular ever since their arrival in Pollington, Mrs. Grimm had of course avoided calling on them. But she was at enmity with the Vicar; therefore as soon as his conduct with regard to the testimonial got wind, she hastened to call on the curate and his sister.

After some very elaborate preliminary civilities, she observed :

' We are all on your brother's side.'

' But my brother says he has no side,' quietly rejoined Margaret. ' He holds that if a curate cannot work amicably with his Vicar he ought to go, and not to stir up strife in the parish.'

Soon after hearing that declaration, Mrs. Horsman Grimm took her departure, and did not trouble the Plaintons with another call.

The people deeply resented the Vicar's

action. Unknown to the curate, several private meetings of the principal parishioners were held, where the matter was eagerly discussed. Hatter had scarcely a friend in the place. There was hardly a lady in the congregation he had not insulted in some one of his strange paroxysms of temper, though it was a very curious thing that he always managed to restrain himself in the presence of their husbands or brothers. Only two persons refrained from condemning his conduct. One of these was Mrs. Sowerby, who, as a matter of duty, always sided with the reigning authority, whatever it might do—she might be considered the layman's exemplification of the great principle so victoriously maintained by the celebrated Vicar of Bray— and the other was Mr. Jervis, who was Mr. Hatter's stock-broker.

Plainton used the most strenuous efforts to remove all ill-feeling on the part of the people towards the Vicar, and in a great measure apparently succeeded. Dr. Jolly and John Bridge, finding how deeply the curate de-

plored the resentment which had been excited, used all their influence—which was not
a little—to get the people to let the matter
drop, and after many weeks' discussion it was
agreed to do so.

'The principal object of our getting up the
testimonial,' observed John Bridge, puffing
away at an enormous meerschaum, ' to relieve
Plainton's mind of any anxiety we could, has
been defeated by the Vicar himself. But,
Scissors and Shears! who would have expected him to act the part of Dick Turpin.
There must be something in the air of the
Vicarage which favours rapacity. Now I
come to think of it, it faces the cross-roads
where the gallows stood in the last century.'

Out of regard to the curate's feelings, the
subject was never referred to in his presence ;
but the Vicar was never able to remove the
deep distrust and suspicion his insatiable
avarice had excited among the members of
his congregation.

Old Mr. Broadbeam elaborated a very
subtle scheme for punishing Hatter. He

proposed to Mr. Thornycroft, his brother magistrate, that they should both call on the Vicar and get up an altercation with him. Then one of them should take hold of him or push him so as to tempt him to resist. When they had got him to do that, they would immediately summon him before themselves for an aggravated assault, and give him two months' imprisonment without the option of a fine. We are glad to state here that this scheme, however admirable for its ingenuity, was finally abandoned.

Many of the wealthiest parishioners withdrew their subscriptions to the parish institutions, and the offertories fell off by one-third of their usual amount.

The effect on the poor was most disastrous. 'The Vicar's a thief,' said old Beets; 'he leave t' curate to do all the work, and when t' people get him up a little lump of money like, t' Vicar comes home, and takes it away. If that ain't a-breaking of eighth commandment, which t' Vicar reads every Sunday, I'm dang'd !'

CHAPTER XV.

A FADING MUSICAL STAR.

ONE Monday morning in June, when Plainton went as usual across to the Vicarage to receive instructions, he found Mrs. Hatter in the drawing-room with Hetty. While Mrs. Hatter was talking to the curate, the child took up a watering-can which her mother had been using for some geraniums in the next room, and began to water the flowers worked in the carpet. She had finished one row before her mother observed her. When she did, she rushed towards her enterprising child and snatched the pot away, leaving, however, the rose of it in Hetty's hands.

'I want to water the flowers,' sobbed the little gardener.

'The flowers in the carpet don't want watering. You may water those in the garden.'

'The garden flowers have had some rain, and the poor flowers in the carpet are quite dry,' continued Hetty, crying as if her heart would break.

'Nonsense, you silly child!'

'Pray, *do* let me water the poor flowers. The ones I have watered are quite fresh now. Look, mamma!—and the others are quite dead.'

'I cannot allow it. You will spoil the carpet.'

'It will make the carpet look quite new. Pray *do* let me water the flowers!' and here Hetty knelt down in front of her mother, clasping her little hands together and looking up piteously into her mother's face with streaming eyes. 'Oh! I *must* water the poor flowers! *Do* let me, I entreat!'

Plainton felt that he could not have resisted such a pathetic appeal, and would have let her water the carpet to her heart's content.

It was less objectionable than tormenting poor Spot.

'Hetty! if you make that noise you shall go to bed!'

Hetty retired to a corner, sobbing bitterly.

'I will tell Mr. Hatter you are here,' said Mrs. Hatter to Plainton, and left the room.

As soon as she was gone Hetty hastily dried her eyes, and muttering in a determined tone, 'I *shall* water the flowers!' took up the watering-pot, and not waiting to put on the rose, which she still held in her hand, recommenced her watering with great zeal.

'You will be put to bed, Hetty,' said Plainton.

'Ha! ha! what do you know about it? You think you are very clever. I'll water you presently, I think!'

Just then her mother returned.

'Oh! Hetty! you naughty child!' snatching away once more the watering-can. But she had not moved more than two paces when Hetty, taking accurate and deliberate aim,

hurled the rose in her mother's face with considerable violence.

Mrs. Hatter hastily dropped the can, which
falling over on its side, speedily discharged the
remainder of its contents upon the unfortunate
carpet. Plainton looked at Mrs. Hatter and
saw a long jagged scratch reaching across her
nose and down the side of her face. She
threw herself into a chair and held the
damaged feature, which happened to be a very
prominent one with Mrs. Hatter, with both
hands.

'Mr. Hatter,' said she, with muffled voice,
' is in his study.'

Plainton made a hasty exit, for he saw that
her nose was bleeding profusely, and was
already much swollen.

The curate finished his business with the
Vicar as quickly as he could, and was coming
away with the usual unpleasant, repellent feeling these interviews always excited in his mind,
when Hatter said :

' Eh—eh—by-the-bye, I wish to make you
a little present, to show my appreciation of

your ungrudging labour on my behalf—eh—
eh—Have you a good bookcase ?'

'No—I manage very well without.'

'How ?'

'I have begged a number of wine-boxes
from my friends, and these I pack sideways,
one above the other, and they answer very well
for shelves.'

'You would not object to receive a bookcase, if I gave you one ?'

'Thank you,' said he, in an embarrassed
tone, 'it is not necessary. I am quite content with my substitute.'

'Eh—eh—but I *wish* to make you a present,' said the Vicar, somewhat angrily, 'and
a handsome bookcase will look better than
common deal boxes.'

'Certainly, it would look better.'

'Well, then, will you go to Mrs. Taylor's
house in Bott's Lane?—you remember she died
whilst I was away. Her daughter is rather
badly off, and would no doubt be glad to sell
some of the furniture. You can look at the
case and see what she will take for it, and

bring the bill to me. I believe it has been in the family a great many years, and from what Humm tells me will require a little doing up. But with a new door, which you could get for a trifle, a couple of new shelves, which might be had for next to nothing, and the judicious application of a little glue and of a little French polish, you could make it look quite a handsome piece of furniture. I should think you might get it for three half-crowns.'

'Thank you very much, but I think I would rather not undertake it. And, indeed, I am not inclined to encumber myself with furniture. Thank you all the same.'

When Plainton saw his sister he said :

'I really think there must be something in the theory of the German philosopher, that every man carries his own atmosphere, which varies in its constituent parts according to the individual character. So that if we could only bottle up each person's atmosphere and analyse it, we should be able accurately to know the moral character without investigating the actual life.'

'That sounds very German, indeed. You have ample material for making experiments of that kind in Pollington.'

'If it be a true theory, the Vicar's character must be a very peculiar one ; for I notice that he carries about him a most uncommon atmosphere, which I can recognise yards away. It was especially active this morning when he was speaking about the bookcase.'

'Oh! you need not go to Germany to find out the cause of that phenomenon. There is a much simpler explanation.'

'Indeed!' said Plainton, wonderingly; 'I should like to know it.'

'The most probable explanation is, that Hatter has not had a bath since the day his nurse gave him one.'

'Really, really!'

'I do not believe in the atmospheric theory of character. Physical causes more easily explain the peculiar phenomena in question. But something of a man's character, or at least of his opinions, may certainly be gleaned from his manners and appearance.'

'Oh ! that is the old-clothes' theory. Do you think now you could write down my theological opinions by examining my attire ?'

' In some degree, though you are not a good instance, I admit. You are so much of an eclectic. The stiff felt hat with cord, which you sometimes wear, is high Ritualistic ; your collar is moderate High Church ; but your coat is too short to be Catholic, and may be termed mild Anglican. Your trousers are rather a puzzle, but are sufficiently cosmopolitan to be dubbed Broad. Following a descending theological scale, your boots ought to be ultra-Protestant, but they fit you too well and move too cleanly to be acceptable to our dear friends of the Church Persecution Society and Anti-Rubric Association. I rather think they must be taken to symbolise your sympathy with lay pursuits and secular recreations.'

' Well, have you quite finished ?'

' I have only to remark further, that it is by your collars that I know when your opinions are becoming unsettled. As soon as your theology requires re-adjusting you feel uncomfortable about your neck, and begin to ask for a new pattern for the collar-maker.'

' My neck is pretty comfortable just now. Well, fairest of women,' said Plainton, rising, ' I must be off to see how that poor man is in the Molton Road.'

' Who is that ?'

' A poor fellow in consumption named Mac-Naught. He was formerly a popular singer at some of the music-halls.'

' Has he sent for you ?'

' No. I heard of his case quite by accident. I believe he refuses to see any clergyman. But I can ask his wife.'

As the curate crossed the Green he met the Vicar going to the post. The latter was still very angry with Plainton for refusing the bookcase ; and as he drew near, the curate could distinguish the changing hues of his face, a sure sign of his being vexed.

' Eh—eh—Mr. Plainton, I forgot to mention one thing this morning. I observed that on Whit-Sunday evening, in giving out the second lesson, you said it was taken from the Acts of the *Holy* Apostles. By what authority,' said he, becoming livid with passion, 'do you venture to call them holy?'

'I have no authority but reverence and custom, though I believe the reading of the book in the Vulgate sanctions the appellation.'

'The Vulgate,' screamed Hatter, stamping his foot, 'has no authority in this Protestant land!'

'Well, if you object to the custom, as you are Vicar, I shall of course respect your wishes.'

'I do object to the apostles being called holy without authority. And every time you give out a lesson from the Acts of the Apostles, and unlawfully use the term "holy" as you did on Sunday, you are guilty of brawling, and are liable to three months' imprisonment!'

Plainton looked at him with somewhat of wonder, and then continued his walk, saying to himself:

'So because I would not chouse a poor woman out of her belongings in order that the Vicar might enjoy the luxury of generosity at a low price, the poor apostles have to suffer ! What a dreadful affliction is a spiteful temper !'

When Plainton arrived at MacNaught's house, he inquired how the man was.

'He is very bad, sir,' said his wife, 'getting weaker every day.'

'Would he like to see me ?'

'I am afraid he would not, sir.'

At that moment the sound of a feeble voice trying to sing issued from the sick man's room.

'Your husband is a singer ?'

'Yes, sir, he mostly amuses himself by singing some of the old songs.'

The poor man was feebly attempting to get through 'Hearts of Oak.' When he came to the chorus, the curate, who was still standing on the door-step, joined in :

> "'Hearts of oak are our ships,
>   Jolly tars are our men ;
>   We always are ready,—
>   Steady, boys, steady !
> We'll fight and we'll conquer again and again !'"

' Polly !' said the voice from within.

' Yes, Joe,' she answered, going in.

' Who's that singing ?'

' Only the curate.'

' Ask him to come in.'

' Will you come in, sir ?'

Plainton went in, and found a man of about fifty years of age, very much wasted away with disease, but still retaining a clear, intelligent eye.

' You sing, sir ?'

' Yes, sometimes.   I am very fond of it.'

' Ah ! so used I to be, but my day is over now.   I like a good old English song still, though I cannot sing it.'

' So do I.'

' Do you know " Tom Bowling "?'

' I am not sure that I can remember all the words.'

' Here they are,' said the man, reaching to Plainton a book which was lying on the bed. ' Perhaps you would not mind singing it.'

' Certainly not, if it will give you any pleasure.'

Plainton accordingly sang ' Tom Bowling.' MacNaught listened with a critical ear.

' Ah ! that suits your sympathetic voice very well. I should say that style suits you better than the patriotic song. Do you know " The Thorn "? '

' Oh yes ; it is a great favourite of mine.'

' I have the words here ; perhaps you will favour the company with it ?'

' Certainly.'

Plainton sang it.

' Ah ! that puts me in mind of old days. I was a public singer once, sir. I hope you won't think the worse of me for that ?'

' Not at all. If you sang the right sort of songs and sang them to the best of your ability, I do not know why you should not be glorifying God in your work as much as other men in theirs.'

' We'll shake hands on that, sir, if you please.'

The curate shook hands with him as desired. After a little more conversation he rose to go.

' Well, sir, I have not had a talk with a

parson since I was a boy. My wife has told
me about you, but I did not know what you
were like, and so I would not have you.
Come again soon.'

On the following Sunday the Vicar invited
Plainton to luncheon. He had now recovered
his equanimity, as the curate had learnt in
the week by the arrival of a portion of the
weekly *Scrutator*. This was always a mark
of Mr. Hatter's goodwill towards his subordinate. If nothing had put him out, he
would send Elijah Humm across to Plainton's
lodgings with such portions of the weekly
oracle as he himself did not want. It usually
came lacking the first three leading articles,
the Occasional Notes, and the notices of new
books. There still remained, however, the
outside sheet, the advertisements, and the
theatrical news.

After luncheon the Vicar invited his curate
on to the lawn.

'Eh—eh—I want to speak to you about
Miss Domville. Don't let her make a fool
of you.'

'Make a fool of me!' exclaimed Plainton in unfeigned astonishment; 'how can she?'

'Eh — eh — she has made fools of two curates already, and will probably try it on with you. She sent one man into a consumption, and the other to the West Indies, which was not much better. She is a great flirt.'

'But I scarcely know her.'

'Eh—eh—she has seven hundred pounds a year. You can't marry a woman without money, as you have none yourself; and if you can really hook her, it would be a very good match.'

'But if I thought of marrying, I could never marry a woman I did not love.'

'Oh!' said Hatter, 'if you think that necessary, I will say no more. We had better go in. It is nearly time for service.'

The next day Plainton went to pay a visit to his old parish. He did not get back till night. When he got in he found the following note:

'" MY DEAR PLAINTON,

'" Mrs. Tadgett, in Bott's Lane, wants her baby baptised. It is ill with the small-pox. Please go at once.

'" Yours,

'" E. H."'

Plainton asked Mrs. Evans when the note came.

'Soon after you left, sir. Mr. Hatter has sent over twice, and the woman herself has been once.'

He hastened round to the house. The poor woman was crying bitterly.

'My poor child is gone, sir. I went twice to the Vicarage, and once to your house, but I could not get any one to come.'

The curate was greatly shocked.

He saw Mr. Hatter the next day. The Vicar was in a great temper.

'There was not a clergyman yesterday to be had in the place,' he said.

'I thought you were at home.'

'So I was, but I cannot spare a moment

from my Pre-Zamzummims. Besides, I never visit infectious cases.'

The curate received no portion of the *Scrutator* that week. Before the following Sunday he gave another look in on Mrs. Tadgett.

'Do you believe, sir,' asked the poor woman, almost as soon as he was inside the house, 'that my child is lost because it was not baptised?'

'God forbid! I know no one who holds such a monstrous theory.'

'I don't believe baptism makes any difference until they are grown up.'

'I cannot go so far as that. Christ has told us to baptise, and it must make a difference whether we do as we are told or not.'

'Yes, sir, it may make a difference to those whose duty it is to do it, but not to the poor child who cannot help it. A baby in arms does not know what is good for itself.'

'You might as well say it does not matter whether a child takes wholesome food or drinks poison, as he does not know any better.

It is not a child's fault when he has heredi-tary disease, it is his misfortune. There may be a cure for the disease, but we cannot cure the child unless we use the cure.'

' What difference, then, sir, do you suppose it makes to my baby who was not baptised, because the Vicar would not come and do it ?'

' I cannot tell. This I know, that the same Father who gave you your child in love, has taken him away again in love. You need not fear. He is in God's hands, who is in-finitely more loving than the most loving mother. You love your child; God loves him a million times more than ever you can, and will do for him all that infinite love can

' I could not bear the thought of never seeing him again !'

' I believe you will see him again, if, when you die, you are good enough to be with one who, like your child, has never sinned ; and you may be this through Christ.'

' I know I have not been as good as I ought.'

'Then, my good woman, begin at once by trying to be what you think you ought to be.'

'My husband will take a drop too much at times, and it puts me out. I lose my temper and then there's a row.'

'Well, begin by trying to keep your temper, and using gentle persuasion to keep your husband from drinking too much.'

'Ah! that's very hard to do, sir.'

'I know it is hard. It is hard to be a Christian at all. I find it very hard at times, but by the help of God I hope to keep on trying to be good, and I trust He will in the long run make me what I cannot make myself,' said Plainton earnestly.

'Don't talk like that, sir,' rejoined the soft-hearted woman, with tears in her eyes, 'as if you wasn't good already. Everybody knows better than that.'

'My good woman, I do try to carry out in my life what I teach in the pulpit, because I believe myself in what I say, but I have many failures.'

'You talk very down-hearted, sir.'

'I did not mean to do that.   I have great reason to rejoice that God has made me of use to some here, and when I have grown much better, I shall be of more use I hope, and shall rejoice the more.'

'Well, sir, I am glad you looked in.   It has made me feel more peaceful like.'

'I am glad of that,' said the curate, smiling, as he shook hands and departed.   He went up the road till he came to MacNaught's.

He found his patient somewhat weaker, but very pleased to see him.

At the man's request he sang to him one or two more old songs.   He found him a very good critic of the words, and after some conversation on this matter he directed his attention to some Biblical Battle and National songs.

The man listened with undisguised interest.

'Now for a descriptive song of victory,' continued Plainton, 'I know nothing more powerful than the song of Moses and Miriam after the passage of the Red Sea.'

'Read it, sir, please.'

The curate read with emphasis the magnificent triumphant ode given in Exodus xv. The man followed his tones with glistening eye, and when, with full voice and animated face, he concluded with the words :

' " Sing ye to the Lord, for He hath triumphed gloriously ; the horse and his rider hath He thrown into the sea ;" ' Mac-Naught feebly waved his hand over his head, and exclaimed with as much force as he could :

'Hurrah ! Rule Britannia ! I remember the story, but it never came home to me like that before. It sounds as if it happened yesterday. Perhaps you can find another.'

'I am afraid I cannot find you a sea song exactly, for the Jews were not a very nautical people, like we are. They never seem to have taken to the sea from a love of danger and adventure. But certainly you get nothing in Dibdin truer to nature than this :' and he read part of Psalm cvii., beginning at the 23rd verse :

' "They that go down to the sea in ships, and occupy their business in great waters." '

' But here is something in a different style. It is a lament for the fallen brave, quite as pathetic as the " Death of Nelson," or " Tom Bowling," ' and he read " David's Song of the Bow," in 2 Sam. i.

' "The beauty of Israel is slain upon thy high places !

' "How are the mighty fallen !" '

' Ah !' said his hearer, ' David was a faithful friend, and a real poet, too !'

' I must be going now, but I will first read to you a national and patriotic song which, considering all the attendant circumstances, is unequalled for sublimity and grandeur. " God save the Queen " looks very small beside it.'

The curate then began to read Rev. v. 9, ending with the words, ' Blessing, and honour, and glory, and power, be unto Him that sitteth upon the throne, and unto the Lamb for ever and ever.'

' That is the national anthem of Heaven, sung in honour of the King of kings, and I

hope that you and I may one day take part
in it.'

On leaving MacNaught's, he looked into the
grounds at the Manor House, and was soon
joined by Maud and Ethel.

'Mr. Plainton, what do you think?' said
the former : 'mamma says we must both go to
school at the end of the summer!'

'Well, I think it will be a good thing for
you—and for me too,' he added, laughing,
'for then I shall have all the park to myself.'

'How naughty of you to say so,' put in
Ethel. 'You will be very sorry not to have us
to take care of you.'

'I dare say I shall miss you.'

'But you are to come and see us,' said
Maud.

'Yes, and you are to write to me ; mamma
says so.'

'Why, you will have to get some one to
read my letters to you if I do.'

'How absurd you are! Come and see
mamma!'

Plainton went in and found that Mrs. Tem-

pleton had had so much trouble in getting a
governess to her mind that she had at length
thought of sending the two children to school,
if she could find a good one. Did Mr. Plainton
know of one ?

The curate mentioned Overshot as having a
school likely to suit, and as being at a convenient distance. Mrs. Templeton determined
to go and see it.

CHAPTER XVI.

THE VICAR IN THE PULPIT.

On the following Saturday Hatter and Plainton attended the consecration of the Church of St. Saviour, Marsden Hill, situated in the adjoining diocese.

As they walked along together the Vicar said :

'Eh—I think I arranged that you should preach in the morning to-morrow ?'

'You did.'

'Well, if it makes no difference to you, I will take the morning sermon and you can take the evening. I want to speak on Baptism, as I find very erroneous views are abroad, and it may be of more use in the morning.'

'Very good.'

After a pleasant walk of half-an-hour they arrived at the church. It had been built chiefly by the subscriptions of a few wealthy families of the neighbourhood. It was intended to be a centre of Evangelical effort. The new Vicar, an amiable and worthy man, was a pronounced Low Churchman of the most uncompromising type. In order to ensure the Evangelical succession in the pastorate, the promoters of the scheme declined to give up the patronage of the living into the hands of the bishop, especially as the Right Reverend Dr. Thwaites Leycester was considered to be rather High. The bishop had of course opposed this plan, but finding that if he persevered in his opposition there was a real danger of the church being opened without consecration in connection with the Free Church movement, he at last consented to consecrate it leaving the patronage in the hands of trustees.

As soon as Plainton entered the vestry, the vicar of the new church, who was an old friend of his, asked :

' Have you brought a long surplice ?'

' I have my own pocket surplice with me.'

' Yes, but is it a *long* one ? Because I am determined not to allow a short surplice to enter the church : for a short surplice is the beginning of the abomination of desolation of Romanism.'

' Oh ! I see !' said his friend, smiling ; ' my surplice comes down to my ankles, and nearly covers my cassock. But you shall see it.'

' My dear fellow, I quite take your word.'

' Thank you,' said Plainton, who was highly amused at this excessive display of Protestant zeal.

At that moment Hatter appeared from the other end of the vestry in a short grubby surplice, which looked as if he had slept in it, and hardly reached his knees. Plainton very mischievously pointed out to the new vicar this appalling breach of his regulations.

' Excuse me for observing that my Vicar appears in a very short surplice indeed. It is positively indecent. Had you not better give him another ?'

' Oh ! no, that's all right, as he does not wear a cassock. I don't mind the congregation seeing his legs as long as they do not see anything approaching a Papistical vestment.'

The Vicar of Pollington had bought a new hat—a rare luxury for him—in which to meet the bishop on this important occasion, and this article of attire he would by no means part with. When the procession was formed from the vestry, he marched up the church in front of the bishop carrying his new silk hat carefully in front of his breast, as if it were the bishop's mitre. When he got within the sacrarium he deliberately placed it down near the front of the table. Unfortunately the vicar-elect, who followed close upon his heels, was short-sighted, and, not seeing the hat, gave it a violent but quite accidental kick which sent it rolling over towards the bishop's chair. The bishop, with great dignity, took it up and handed it to the verger over the rails.

Dr. Leycester preached the sermon, in which he gave a very severe rebuke to the

promoters of the church, not only for the part
they had taken in opposing the usual arrangements as to patronage, but in assigning the
most uncomfortable seats in the church to the
poor.   He quoted, with great effect, Sir
Samuel Romilly as to the law of England on
this point.   It was an able sermon, and delivered with great force and dignity.

Plainton knew Dr. Leycester slightly, and
rather admired the man.   There was a
romance connected with his early days, the
particulars of which he had heard from a connection of the family.   But there was no trace
of softness or sentiment in his lordship's face,
which was strongly lined and indicated extreme fixity of purpose.   His manner, however, was exceedingly courtly and gracious,
and the hardness of the strong face was re-
deemed by the striking melodiousness of his
voice, which he knew how to modulate to a
nicety.

There was the usual confusion in the vestry when the service was ended.   Whilst the
bishop was signing the preacher's book an

odd incident occurred. Three or four peas from an invisible shooter struck him sharply in the face. He quickly looked up, when another fierce volley caused him hastily to turn aside. Rubbing his nose with his handkerchief, he exclaimed to the new vicar :

'What is the meaning of this, Mr. Latimer? Dear me! this is exceedingly painful! Very painful and unexpected!'

The cause was soon discovered. Hetty had been brought to the church by the maid, and whilst the latter was holding a pleasant conversation with a male friend, and making an appointment for Sunday evening, Hetty had wandered into the vestry. Not quite approving of the bishop's face and of the attention which he seemed to arrogate to himself, she had pulled out her pea-shooter—one of her favourite toys—and fired the charges in rapid succession which had so greatly disturbed his lordship's equanimity. Hatter quickly carried off his enterprising child into the church, while Mr. Latimer, who knew Hetty only too well, with much circumlocu-

tion explained the origin of the incident.
Plainton had expected that Dr. Leycester
would be very angry, but he was agreeably
surprised to see the worthy bishop turn round
—though still rubbing his nose—and, with a
smile, ask for the child with the pea-shooter.
But she did not return, nor did Hatter.

Plainton stayed to the luncheon, which was
given by one of the trustees of the church.
He was not very pleased with the conversation at the table.   It seemed to him that his
brother clergy were too much engrossed by
domestic cares and incidents, and too much
influenced by their women-folk.   Very probably it may have seemed so to him, as his
thoughts of late had been intently fixed upon
the probable future of the Church, and he
had been absorbed with the consideration as
to whether it was or was not desirable that in
large and densely-populated districts, such as
the East-end of London, the priesthood
should be celibate.

When he heard one clergyman, an Irish-
man, eulogise the ladies extravagantly, and

affirm that nothing in the Church could be done without them, he asked himself if this were a wise and dignified speech to make in mixed company.

Again, when an incumbent on his left hand began to tell him that his wife had been confined on the previous day and was doing well, Plainton certainly thought that the clergy were forcing the ladies into unwholesome prominence, and exhibiting themselves rather as official subordinates to that dangerous and mysterious sex, than as its leaders and rulers.

It is likely that the curate would have taken a more lenient view had he mixed more freely with his clerical brethren. But when not engaged in the duties of his office, he spent a good deal of his spare time (such as he had) in solitary thought and speculation, which was probably the reason why the conversation at the luncheon so strongly jarred upon his feelings.

When the bishop was leaving the table to fulfil another engagement in the neighbourhood, he was accidentally tripped up by Mrs.

Latimer's long train, and nearly fell against the chair. Recovering himself, he bowed low to that much-embarrassed lady and said :

' I beg your pardon, Mrs. Latimer. It was quite my fault—' suddenly appearing to recollect himself, he added, with his proverbial love of accuracy, 'but partly yours—partly yours. Those long trains are a great mistake. I have tried to stop them in my own family, but not with perfect success.'

With this careful statement of facts he took a kindly leave.

The next day Hatter took the pulpit in the morning, as he had arranged on the road to St. Saviour's. He was a good preacher. Plainton honestly admired his intellectual power as displayed in his sermons, although it was not often he agreed with his opinions. As he was so able a preacher and needed not to fear any rivalry from his curate, Plainton was the more surprised that he should at times manifest so much petty spite against himself in connection with the pulpit work.

The curate always knew when he had preached what the Vicar considered a particularly able or effective sermon, for Mr. Hatter made himself extremely disagreeable for the rest of the week. He would take great pains to show Plainton that his doctrine was unsound, or his views dangerous in their tendency, or his exposition inaccurate. Failing these, he would say, as if he himself had not been present and heard it :

' I hear you preached a particularly good sermon on Sunday. Eh—eh—that is to say, the people liked it. It was about up to their level, I think. They cannot take in much, and approve of anything that is florid and in the *Daily Phonograph* style.'

Then he would pluck his beard and furtively watch the effect of his speech on Plainton's face. But the curate soon got used to this mode of attack, and knowing what it meant, generally received it with stolid indifference. Sometimes, however, he was so tickled by the Vicar's display of petty temper that he would burst out laughing, and reply that he was glad his preaching was suited to the people he addressed.

Hatter tried very often to get Plainton to say whether he liked preaching best in the morning or evening, and to ascertain if he was very anxious to take the pulpit when he could be released by the accidental arrival of one of the Vicar's friends. Plainton knew from experience that if he expressed a particular liking for any one kind of work, his amiable Vicar would endeavour to give him as little of it as possible, and set him on to something which he might suppose would be less agreeable. So with regard to preaching, he knew that if he showed preference for any one time, Mr. Hatter would take good care that another should fall to his lot. He therefore carefully avoided expressing any special liking for any one kind of work, or for any particular time in which to do it. Whatever was assigned to him he was willing to do to the very best of his ability ; but he was very unwilling to do it and also to be badgered because he had done it.

Hatter's sermons were generally acute, logical, and ingenious, except he preached in a temper, when he was ingenious and spiteful, but neither logical nor acute. He was seldom original, but always interesting. He had the useful faculty of putting the thoughts of others in a simple and attractive dress. Very often his sermons were spoiled by his special pleading, specious reasoning, and love of paradox. Frequently he would audaciously state a half truth as if it were the whole. He possessed a silvery, though not a strong voice, which made certain portions of his sermons very effective. He was, however, a great plagiarist, and constantly, without acknowledgment, preached as his own large portions of the sermons of Maurice, Kingsley, F. W. Robertson, Brookfield, and Stopford Brooke ; and adaptations from the Essays of Matthew Arnold.

But perhaps his greatest defect was his misquoting of Scripture, which he did to suit his argument in the most unblushing manner. Fred Monmouth maintained that his scholar-

ship was in many respects inaccurate and unsound, and Fred Monmouth, who was a well-
known Oxford examiner, and a classic of rare
ability, was a man who knew what he was
saying.

Another of his eccentricities was his habit
of replying to his curate's sermons Sunday
after Sunday. This was no doubt highly
amusing to the intellectually combative portions of the congregation, but hardly satisfying
to those who longed to have their doubts re-
solved and their faith strengthened.

If Plainton preached on the Atonement,
the Vicar on the following Sunday would show
there was nothing in it, and that sin was a
natural disorder which would in time right
itself. His favourite saying in connection
with this subject was, that ' it was easier for
Christ to die than to be born,' which might or
might not be true, but in its application was
misleading.

If Plainton spoke of the duty of aspiring to
a life of holiness, the Vicar would broadly hint,
when his innings in the pulpit came round,

that a man who used such expressions was a
hypocrite, and that whilst our Lord forgave
the woman taken in adultery, He denounced
in the bitterest terms the hypocritical Pha-
risees who were always trying to make themselves righteous.

It was customary, also, for Mr. Hatter to
make allusions in his sermons more or less
pointed to circumstances which might have
occurred in the parish in the previous week.
This was no doubt in many respects a useful
plan. But Plainton was somewhat astonished
at the way in which he referred to incidents
in which the preacher himself had been an
actor, and had not come out of them very
creditably.

If he had given way to a violent fit of
temper, or shown ill-will to any of his congregation, when Sunday came round he would
preach an affecting sermon on meekness,
amiability, and patience under insults.

If he had been guilty of any act particularly
mean or selfish, he would preach strongly and
earnestly on self-sacrifice as the law of the

life of God.   When for instance he took possession of the curate's testimonial, and the
congregation resented it, with trembling voice
and streaming eyes he urged on them the
loveliness of generosity, as being a higher principle than that of justice.   In this particular
case the curate would have been satisfied with
justice if he could have obtained it, and would
have preferred to dispense with the peculiar
generosity displayed by the Vicar.

   Fred Monmouth remarked that Hatter
knew his duty if he could not do it, and might
have concluded most of his sermons with the
precept, 'Do as I say, but not as I do.'
Oftentimes, while listening to his preaching,
the words of Ophelia to Laertes would rise
up in the curate's mind :

> 'Do not, as some ungracious pastors do,
>   Show me the steep and thorny way to heaven ;
>   Whilst, like a puff'd and reckless libertine,
>   Himself the primrose path of dalliance treads,
>   And recks not his own read.'

The Vicar's sermon on baptism was much
liked by some, and especially by the non-

communicating portion of the congregation.

The next day as Fred Monmouth was walking towards the railway station he was over-
taken by Mr. Chubb, who, after exchanging
civilities, remarked :

' Capital sermon from the Vicar yesterday
—one of his best. That's the sort of thing I
like from the pulpit—something you can
understand—no making the Sacraments into
some incomprehensible mystery like Plainton
does—a lot of hocus-pocus to bogey old
women with. It was most original.'

' I am not so sure about its originality,'
mildly replied Monmouth ; ' it might be considered in some degree original in the way
in which it was preached by Robertson at
Brighton, though that kind of argument is
almost as old as Christianity itself, but I can
hardly look upon it as in any sense original
when preached by Hatter.'

' What ! you don't mean to say that it was
not his own ?'

' It was his own so far as ink and paper

were concerned, but that is all. Here '—pulling out of his pocket Robertson's second series of sermons—' I have promised to lend this to John Bridge and then to Dr. Jolly, but you will have time to glance at the two sermons on baptism whilst we walk to the station, if you are going so far.'

Chubb hastily glanced at the sermons indicated. He recognised sentence after sentence of the preceding Sunday's discourse. Then he looked carefully at the concluding paragraphs, and not finding Hatter's eloquent and fervid peroration, delivered with trembling voice and uplifted arm, he exclaimed triumphantly :

'Yes, yes, that's quite allowable. The greatest writers and thinkers freely use the thoughts of other men. Look at Shakespeare, now : he took the rubbishing plays and stories of nobodies, and by his genius made them immortal. That peroration of the Vicar's— where he began to speak of the torn flag which——'

'Oh! you mean the blackened bit of old

rag. You will find that in the middle of the second sermon—pistol-shots and all. There it is. Yes, Hatter flourishes the old rag with considerable effect at times. But I think it sounded quite as well the first time he used it.'

' I never heard it before,' said Chubb in a discomfited tone.

' No ? I think you were out fishing on the two occasions to which I refer,' said Monmouth, calmly; ' he always thrusts the blackened bit of old rag in our eyes when he has been showing that the doctrines of the Church are untenable. For instance, when he explains away the Real Presence, or the gift at Confirmation, or in Holy Orders, he is obliged to pull out of his pocket the blackened bit of old rag to make amends. But here's my train. Bye-bye.'

The Davenports did not often come to church, but when they did they brought a large following of members of Parliament, and other well-known personages, who might be staying with them at Acacia Vale.

When Hatter knew of the Secretary being in the parish he would prepare a special sermon for him. One which he had carefully prepared for this purpose he brought to church four times without letting off, as Mr. Secretary was not present. He used instead an alternative discourse which he had put in his pocket to provide for such a contingency.

At last Mr. Davenport made his appearance, and the Vicar launched his bolt, or rather it would be a more appropriate figure to say, he spread his lime. For it was a clever sermon, in which the well-known scientific views of the Secretary were skilfully and delicately advocated. The inspiration of the Bible was not absolutely denied, but the stress laid upon the inspiration which dictated secular works seemed to exalt the latter to a level with the former. It was precisely the kind of sermon which would captivate a cultured, worldly man, who was very much of a free-thinker, and rejected altogether the doctrinal teaching of the Church.

The Vicar was so highly pleased with his

performance that he invited Plainton to luncheon immediately after, and gave him not only a portion of the *Scrutator*, but lent him an old number of the *Pall Mall Gazette*.

During the week Mr. Hatter received a five-pound note from Mr. Davenport for the parish charities, and what he much more highly valued, an invitation to dinner. When he returned home after the latter he told Mrs. Hatter that supposing Dr. Cartwright, who was the present Rector of Cunningstone (a rich living in the gift of Earl Greyling), did not die soon, he had great hopes that he had hooked the interest of Mr. Secretary Davenport, who was quite the fourth ablest man in the Cabinet, and had considerable ecclesiastical influence.

Our readers will remember the alarm of Margaret on discovering that the movements of herself and her brother were watched by an unknown observer. Since that night Plainton had carefully kept a look-out for the man, but had failed to see him again. Margaret, however, thought she saw him once or twice on the other side of the road, but he made off when she looked round. He was so muffled up that she had not seen his face.

On the Sunday following the events just related, the curate and his sister went to sup with the Broughams, and to have a few hymns after the day's heavy work.

As they walked home through the Grove, Margaret said to her brother in a low tone:

' We are followed again !'

Plainton listened, and heard footsteps a few yards behind.

' Wait till we get by the lamp, and then I will look round,' he whispered.

They walked slowly on, and when they were a few paces past the lamp, Plainton suddenly turned about. He saw what he thought was the same figure he had seen on the night of Margaret's alarm, but he could not be sure. The man had his neck muffled up—although the night was quite warm—and wore a wide-awake hat. He turned short off across the road just before reaching the lamp.

Plainton waited, but the man crossed into the Molton Road and disappeared.

' It is very strange,' said Plainton. ' Have you seen him lately ?'

' Only once or twice, when we have been out rather late, but then he seemed very anxious to avoid us, and I did not say anything about it, as you did not.'

' I think it is the same man who alarmed you at first.'

' I am sure of it.'

' Then the next time he follows us I will know who he is and what he means.'

END OF VOL. I.

HILLING AND SONS, PRINTERS, GUILDFORD, SURREY.

www.ingramcontent.com/pod-product-compliance
Lightning Source LLC
Chambersburg PA
CBHW030814020726
47499CB00006B/1910